A Second Chance for Eve?

Precious in the sight of the LORD
is the death of his saints. Psalm
116:15

I0589895

Written by
Nathan L. Gavin

2020 EDITION

HAVE YOU EVER done something that had catastrophic results? Do you wish that you had a second chance, a 'do-over' to right that wrong? Could Adam and Eve have felt that same way? Christ was said to be that do-over, **or the second man Adam**. Would Eve be given a second chance at redemption ? And if so, who would be worthy to redeem her?

TABLE OF CONTENTS

Special Thanks

TO MY PARENTS, Charles and Lucille, thanks for showing me how to be a responsible young man. I will never forget all the life lesson that you have taught me. Mom, your prayers got me through so many hard times. Dad your stern but loving hands guided me and helped me stay on the right path. You both lead by example! I love you. Rest in Heaven. To my immediate family and friends who are like family, thank you for all your love and support.

To my late pastor, Dr. Rosemary Cosby better known as (Mama), thank you for all that you did for me while you were with us. You taught me how to pray and to discover a personal relationship with God, who then revealed to me his son. Your exceptionally holy life set a standard by which we can live. I will never forget you, and I will meet you in the city called heaven!

Special thanks to the following people for helping me with the completion of this book:

To my wife Jen, I could have never made it through without you.

Countless hours were spent on my computer, and the library,sometimes meetings, and you picked up the slack and took care of the family. Your insight and confirmations that I was supposed to write this book helped move forward with this project. I am so excited to share this journey and the rest of my life with you.

Deborah, Diana, Dana, and Arlinda. my crew, we started this journey together and saw it through to the end. I couldn't have made it through without your support, encouragement, and monetary gifts.

Deborah, you have been my right hand, and God sent people to you that played a major part in furthering the progression of this book.

Tom Z, when I started, I had an idea, a pen, paper and no direction. You brought it out of me. You took jumbled and crumpled pieces of paper and created a masterpiece. All the hard work you did with editing and proofreading was time-consuming and took you from your family. I'm forever grateful.

Sam K, your insight, and creativeness have blown me away. You are amazingly talented and gifted. Thanks for your true support and brutal honesty. Sometimes a person doesn't need a pat on the back, but instead a dose of reality and constructive criticism to perfect a project.

Kelly O, your books are amazing. You have a spiritual connection with your audience. I was excited when you wrote about God sending a writer to you for help, and then I appeared. Talk about a confirmation and blessing. Thanks for inspiring me to want to achieve more.

I have been inspired by many childhood/church friends. A lot of you have become authors, business owners, motivational speakers, professional athletes and actors /actresses. This reassured me that with hard work and dedication, your dreams can become your reality!

Nate L. Galvin

Forward

WHEN MY HUSBAND asked me to write a forward, I was seriously hesitant. My passion has always been in health care and taking care of others not writing. But who better to speak about my husband than I. From the first day I met him in church (he is a minister), I noticed that he had a gift of speaking to others. For some reason, people are drawn to him and often come to him for advice.

I also notice that he had a passion for writing. By the way he would write letters for business purposes and school projects, but I would have never guessed he would ever become, or had the desire to become an author.

Early one morning my husband woke up with this idea to write a book. I was shocked but wanted to be supportive . Sometime later I got a confirmation when I heard God's voice say that your husband will have a great calling and that I would have to support him through this. Nate told me that this was the reassurance that he was looking for to proceed.

I feel that there is a message in this book that he needs to share with the world. And regardless of how successful this book becomes, I want him to know that me, our kids, and families are very proud of him.

Jen Galvin

More About the Author

THE AUTHOR, NATHAN Galvin, grew up in a household with nine siblings and an extended family of nieces and nephews. He is the second youngest sibling. Nathan loved his parents and was particularly fond of his mother, Lucille. I guess you could say he was sort of a "mama's boy" growing up. He cared for his parents until their passing in 2013 and 2016. He was devastated by the loss of his parents but determined to continue their legacy of faith, giving, and embracing everyone they encountered.

Nathan was an interesting kid. He was a little rebellious and was no stranger to the principal's office in elementary school. He was very protective of his siblings, particularly his sisters and nieces, and most of the visits to the principal's office were because he was protecting them.

Nathan grew up attending a small Pentecostal church in Salt Lake City, founded by an African-American woman by the name of Dr. Rosemary Redmond Cosby. Mama, as she was affectionately called, was a powerful woman of God who had a significant impact on Nathan's childhood, and later his decision to join the ministry.

In 2013, Nathan believed that he received a message from God that he was to write a book. This book, although fictional, may reveal a mystery that the world has yet to discover. The author believes that God has always intended to use male and female to portray his image. The author's religious background, and his adoration for his female pastor gave him the courage to write this book. "A Second Chance for Eve" is sure to be controversial, as it contradicts modern-day theology, but this book has its roots in biblical truths.

Deborah Jones

Nathan Lewis, or "Nate Nate," as he is affectionately known, was always doing something. He was the baby boy of the family, but his personality was bigger than most. He fought with everyone, and I mean EVERYONE. He often found himself in trouble at school. I once heard our mother say as she headed up to the school to meet with the principal once again, "Why can't he just go to school and act right like the other kids?" What we didn't realize at the time was that this would be good for him to not be like the other kids. Nate got married and became a young father. To my surprise, he was such a good father. He and his first wife divorced while the boys were still very young. I watched Nate become the ultimate single dad. He always took care of them and put their needs before his own. I was amazed at the patient and caring father he was. Later, when our parents started to get up in age and their health declined, he was one of the first to be there to take care of them. He did so with humor and grace, all while taking care of his family, which now includes a new wife and two more children.

Nate is a very spiritual person and has always shown great faith. As my father-in-law was passing from this life, Nate was the first family member I called for to pray with us. His loyalty is unwavering. I have watched him pour his heart into this book, and I know that if nothing else, God, along with Mom and Dad, are smiling down on him.

Arlinda Jackson

Introduction

ORIGINALLY FROM IDAHO, I wanted to expand my horizons and see other parts of this great country. Growing up in a small city where everyone seemed to know each other made me feel like everything in my life was one-sided or scripted, if you will. I had friends that graduated and married their high school sweethearts, attended the same church, and all seemed to migrate to the same neighborhood. I wanted more. I wanted to explore and learn more about life. After graduation and much research, I had my sights set on Nazareth College, located in Pittsford, a suburb of Rochester, New York. Having a very religious mother when I was growing up, I knew what she believed. But I wanted to see what others opinions were. I knew this was the college for me because it offered a great education, affordability, and classes of a theological nature. Unlike most secular colleges, students can partake in religious studies as a part of their curriculum.

Attending school in New York a few years after 9-11 was an amazing but scary time in my life. However, I was excited about the change. Two years into my college studies, my life would change forever! And as much as I wanted to forget these experiences, they seemed to be etched in my brain. Although I never thought of myself as a religious person by any means, I was left to wonder if these fortuitous dreams somehow meant something more. More than just the ordinary dream.

A Mother's Heartbreak

AS I WATCHED my son sleep, I began to recall many different aspects of his life. You see, both my husband and I thought we were done having children. But we ended up with a pleasant surprise. Charlie, the youngest of our three, had the hardest time coming into this world. At the time of his birth, the doctors had an extremely challenging time trying to deliver him. He was almost 11 lbs. with broad shoulders. His left shoulder was fractured during birth. The doctor was sure that he would never use his arm again. His father and I were devastated when we heard the news, and we broke down and cried for days. All we could do was pray; I just couldn't accept what the doctors were telling me. After a week, we returned for our scheduled follow-up. As the physician was about to examine his shoulder, Charlie began to raise his left hand up in the air. I will never forget the look on the doctor's face when this happened. What took place was nothing short of a miracle. I know that miracles happen every day, but I felt that he was meant to be here and he would need the use of both arms. His healing was reassurance that after such a troubled pregnancy and delivery, the pain that I went through, was all worth it. I just knew that he would be special. Some called it a mother's love. But somehow, I knew better.

He grew up with two siblings and had a pretty normal childhood. Charlie struggled a bit socially through grade school; he was just so shy at times. I was worried that he wouldn't make many friends, but he did just fine. Sometimes he claimed that his left arm was weaker when trying to do pull-ups in gym class, because of what happened at birth, but many of his friends would say after a game of dodge-ball that all the power transferred to his right one.

Soon, we realized that Charlie was just a little bit 'different.' I mean, you never want to make distinctions between any of your children because you love each of them the same. Because he was the baby of the family, he received a little more attention. Charlie did things differently. He seemed to focus on one thing and wouldn't give up until he was able to decipher even the most complex of word puzzles and games. I can still remember as plain as day how he would look on the map and inquire about New York or Washington D.C., and then ask us why we always took vacations to the West Coast and never to the East. Children just don't understand that sometimes it costs more money to travel farther. I knew then that Charlie had a fondness for the East Coast and dreamed of living there someday. I feel blessed to be a mother to all my children.

They've had their share of problems, but they all somehow endured and have gone on to lead rewarding and fulfilling lives. As a mother, I couldn't be prouder.

But Lord, I can't help, but wonder was it all for nothing? With everything that I went through bringing him into this world, how did life take such a drastic turn? I feel so helpless right now. If I ever needed your help before, I sure could use it now.

The Dreams

When it all Started, In My Words.

IT WAS A Saturday morning when I awoke to the sound of rain crashing on my side window. I can remember being angry because I was deep into another recurring dream. "Dang it," I yelled I couldn't believe it happened again. I thought back to the four similar dreams that had taken place; this was the fifth and by far the most intense. I was so close to seeing the face of the woman on the throne. I began having strange dreams periodically over the course of a year. These series of dreams left me clueless as to what they meant. And I was no closer to understanding the meaning of them, or why I would have them.

Sometimes in the early morning hours, as I lay fast asleep, my dream would change. I mean, I could start out dreaming about summer and playing in the park. Or flying on a plane, and out of nowhere, visions of women would appear in them. I can recall looking at these women for what seemed like forever while my brain tried to process who they were, or where they came from. Each time they appeared, they were off in the distance before they came into focus.

The dream that started it all was about a woman standing at the entrance of a beautiful garden. Suddenly there was fire—it was chasing her. She ran as fast as she could, and the fire followed but never consumed her. As she stopped, she looked to be in great pain. I wondered if she were burned? Then she began to act like a woman in labor. She dropped to the ground, clutching her abdomen, breathing heavily and screaming with intense pain. I saw a snake crawling from behind her, and it drew closer as if it were about to strike. Perhaps it had already bitten her, and that was the source of her pain? But then a man appeared and hit the snake in the head, and it retreated off into the grass. He then picked her up and carried her off into a wooded area opposite of where the snake fled. They constantly looked back at the fire in the distance as if the realization was sinking in that they were leaving something important behind, and the woman began to cry.

In the next dream, I saw a woman standing on a mountaintop. She was wearing a white robe with a hood that covered her face. I noticed that there were white sheep off in the distance and a bright light that overshadowed her. Was the light a reflection off her white robe? As I tried to focus, I heard her weeping and saw that she was holding some clothing. The clothing was partially folded, and there seemed to be a vibrant red stain on the garment. Was it wine—or maybe blood? My dream shifted, and I no longer recognized the surroundings. I saw a desert and a lamb. This lamb just lay bleeding. The same woman stood over the lamb and then knelt, still weeping. I tried to focus my eyes even harder but the image never became any clearer, nor did the woman ever reveal her face.

The third dream occurred a few months later. And very much like the first two, there was no specific pattern or clarity. As I started to remember the third one, I went into a deep thought—almost as if it were a state of meditation. I remember seeing bright lights, almost too bright to the human eye. Somehow, for reasons unknown, I could see beyond them. As I continued to look at the light, a white mist appeared. Off in the distance I could see a stream of colors. They were the most beautiful colors I have seen in my life. There were colors I haven't seen on this earth. I was so intrigued by all of this; my curiosity got the best of me. I wanted to see more, learn more. Trying once again to focus, I saw a massive table prepared for a grand celebration. I could see fruit and crystal clear glasses filled with red liquid. On each end of the table sat a crown with all kinds of stones, such as rubies, diamonds, and sapphires. To whom could they belong? As I looked up, my eye caught a glimpse of a beautiful display of colors that hovered over a bright light. Except for this time, I saw two smaller, yet equally bright lights that seemed to stream from opposite sides of the display. It was so bright in this place that no other lighting was necessary. It felt like I was floating in midair, feeling timeless ageless, peaceful, and very calm. I wondered to myself, Is this some type of kingdom? Am I having a near death experience? I also remember thinking I've read about different kings and queens throughout history and seen them in movies maybe this is why it looked so familiar.

The bright lights were getting bigger and brighter. Was I getting closer? Suddenly I stopped. I could not believe what I was seeing. There were three seats: one large and two smaller ones on either side. The seats appeared to be gold in color. Two figures were suddenly somewhat visible. I saw the same crowns that sat on the table now atop their heads. But for some reason the large seat never revealed anyone; I just felt a presence, as if someone was watching me the whole time. This moment right here right now feels amazing, simply amazing. I was in astonishment. In the back of my mind, I thought, are these crowns meant for royalty? But it seemed so stereotypical to think like that. Both these figures were adorned in white, the whitest white that I had ever seen. Am I witnessing a miracle? An unveiling, or a secret of some sorts? Feeling so numb at that moment, I drifted in amazement. Then I began asking myself, who could they be?

Overcome with emotion, I wanted to wake up, scream, yell, or something, but I couldn't. The scene was overwhelming, so I tried focusing on one seat at a time. I looked at what would be the right side of the large seat to notice a male figure with broad shoulders and facial hair. Does he resemble Christ? Oh, that is crazy! I thought. Turning away from the eat on the right, I set my sights on the second seat; things still weren't obvious. Could that be another king? Or perhaps his son? I could notice a slight visible difference. This figure, having the silhouette of breasts and long curly hair. I wondered if I was looking at a queen? Perhaps a female angel of sorts? It didn't look like your typical angel that you may see in a book or on T.V. She never revealed any visible wings. Growing up, I still recall mother telling stories to her friends about angels. Of course, I never really paid much attention to that kind of stuff. I still couldn't shake that unexplainable feeling of awe. It was all so confusing to me, and my thoughts swirled around in my head. Then, just like every other time and just as abruptly, I woke up.

I sat straight up in bed and began fanning myself, pulling off my shirt and letting the air cool me off. I was still in disbelief. Did that just happen? I felt the need to check to see if I was still alive. Still, dizzy from all the excitement, I knew that there would be no going back to sleep.

What was the meaning of that dream? At that moment, I felt 'terrified.' With so many questions and so few answers, I had to jump out of bed and watch T.V to take my mind off everything. An hour later I was on the internet reading about crowns, thrones, angels, and what they symbolized. Almost every site talked about them belonging to royalty, and a few mentioned Christ. Was that who I saw in the first chair?

I let my mind wander on those thoughts and then continued reading the article. It said that Christ had a crown of thorns placed on his head and that he would wear a crown in heaven. Then I turned my focus to women in the Bible who could wear crowns as well. There were plenty of women in the Bible, but my searching yielded no clues as to who could have been seated on the other throne or why there was crown atop her head and on the table.

It was a few months later, and without any reason, I dreamed of another woman. This dream, however, was different. It was in a modern-day classroom setting. I was sitting in the back of the class, taking notes. There were several strange things about this dream. First, I seemed to be the only student there, and although I was writing things down, the teacher was facing the chalkboard. It wouldn't have been so strange, except she never turned around. I wondered if all I would see the whole time was her back. She dressed in professional attire, black skirt and a white blouse. Her hairstyle seemed to resemble one from the late fifties or early sixties. Is this lady my mom or grandma? Is that why I'm seeing her? Taking a closer look, I noticed streaks of gray throughout. I realized that she would be older than my mother, and she had a much lighter complexion than Granny. Who on earth could she be? As she stepped away from the chalkboard, I noticed she was wearing glasses, but other parts of her face were obstructed by the large ruffles on her blouse and the paper she was holding up. She then moved farther away from the board, and I saw that she had written biblical scriptures upon it. Some were in English, and then some were in a different language. Now things were getting strange.

Once again, I awoke, in the middle of the dream but not as abruptly as the last two times. I didn't give this dream much thought because it seemed to be just a "dream." I returned to sleep almost immediately.

Several months passed before I had my final dream about these women. This dream was by far the most intense. I can only describe it as a take-your-breath-away kind of moment. I found myself looking at a throne again, but this time, I was standing right before the woman. Her face was somewhat transparent, but I remembered getting a glimpse of her smiling. It was such a beautiful, warm, and welcoming smile. It was as if she were welcoming me home all with just a smile. I stood there silent as she began to speak.

"I have come through many struggles. Soon the mystery of God will be finished!"

Not wanting to blink, I hoped she would say more. I saw the crown upon her head and realized that she wasn't just an ordinary woman. There was something extraordinary about her. I tried forming words, but just like that, the figure began to disappear. Then as quickly as she had appeared, she went.

I bolted upright, my heart pounding heavily. What had I seen? There was

17

no going back to sleep this time, I'm up now!

"Mystery? What mystery?" I thought about what she had said to me. What does it mean by the mystery of God will soon be finished? Are we at the end of days? When did the mystery of God begin? So many questions, but I realized that these could be more than just dreams now. Somehow, they were different! Would I ever receive some answers? (Or go back to sleep, for that matter.)

Even though I thought about these dreams often, I was splitting my time between school and work. I knew that I needed to focus my attention elsewhere.

My College Experiences

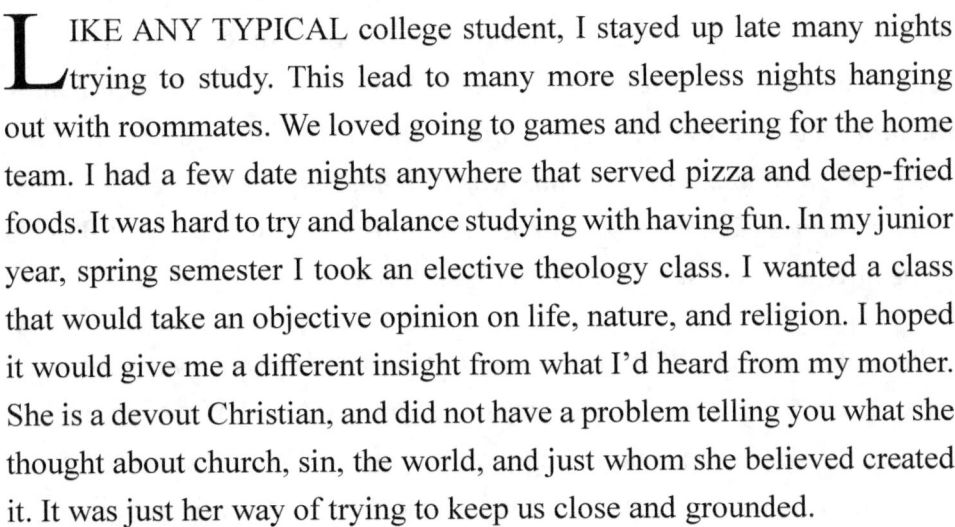

LIKE ANY TYPICAL college student, I stayed up late many nights trying to study. This lead to many more sleepless nights hanging out with roommates. We loved going to games and cheering for the home team. I had a few date nights anywhere that served pizza and deep-fried foods. It was hard to try and balance studying with having fun. In my junior year, spring semester I took an elective theology class. I wanted a class that would take an objective opinion on life, nature, and religion. I hoped it would give me a different insight from what I'd heard from my mother. She is a devout Christian, and did not have a problem telling you what she thought about church, sin, the world, and just whom she believed created it. It was just her way of trying to keep us close and grounded.

This class would turn out to be everything that I had hoped it would be. I can recall looking over the class syllabus; Professor Karen Hartford drew our attention to the final project that would account for 45% of our grade in this class. I wanted to do a great job on this one, and I'm sure that many of my classmates felt the same way. Our professor proposed that students write an essay on either 'Church vs. State or 'Proof of religion or science' Students were to present which side could provide more evidence of its need for existence and relevance. Was there too much involvement of one with the other? I was baffled, and being the worrier that I am wanted to get an early start on this project.

The semester seemed to fly by and Prof. Hartford's class was by far my favorite. We discussed a broad range of religious subjects; there was such a difference of opinion between us that it made things very interesting. I learned a lot from my classmates. Many of them grew up with religious parents, so they understood where I was coming from and why I had so many questions about religion.

Ah, the much-anticipated final project and I'm wondering how in the world I would be able to support this thesis. I knew what I'd heard growing up, and what I had read and even felt. But putting those thoughts and emotions on paper would prove to be most difficult. After much deliberation, I settled on the topic of religion and science. I wondered, *How can I show the differences between the two if there were any? I also pondered about the creation of humanity and this world. What purpose do we serve, and what role does each of us play in this great big movie we call life? Why do some have so much while others have so little?*

I thought to myself, *"Can we argue that God didn't have anything to do with the creation of man?"* Perhaps it was simply an act of evolution? Did man evolve from apes and learn to walk upright? Could that be the case? If so then who created apes? I wanted so badly to get an understanding and be able to convey it to my classmates.

I found myself filled with a range of emotions, from excitement to anxiety. Researching had always been one of my strong suits, but I would need to compile plenty of facts to support both sides and somehow apply my findings to the essay. Easier said than done; I foresaw getting writer's block. Struggling day after day, I continued to write down facts, cite my sources, and try and make sense of it all.

After filling a 'wastebasket' with crumbled remnants, I inserted my flash drive and started to write. When summarizing my final project, I borrowed a quote from Shakespeare's Hamlet and named my paper "To Be or Not to Be." I started by stating how many people would postulate that science and religion are either "to be or not to be" On the one hand, you can state that God had intended for religion 'to be' and for science 'not to be.' On the other, some would say the inverse, that their theories are 'to be' and the existence of a higher power is 'not to be.'

In Sunday school I was the kid who presented controversy to the group. Although we read about God and his son Jesus I wanted to know more about them. Did they exist? Who created the world? Who wrote the Bible?

Who created God? How is it that a spirit, or mass, could have always existed? Does he have a mother or father? These kinds of questions drove my teacher crazy but made for interesting discussions. Boy, those were the good old days. It sure has been awhile since I ventured into a church, primarily because my mother stopped making me go as I got older. Although those dreams made me feel inspired, I'm not sure if the inspiration is of a divine nature or just some crazy feelings that we all get from time to time. As I began to take science classes in high school, I had even more questions especially when I read that man descended from apes. I studied the evolution chart that showed graphs of several apes then eventually the ape turning into a man. But of course, I had to be the one who stirred the pot by asking my teacher, "If a man came from an ape, then why there are still apes?" I got a thunderous applause followed by roaring laughter from the class, but one upset and somewhat baffled teacher. I think a part of me sought out for attention and reactions from people (or perhaps it helped me not be so shy) and the other part of me was curious about what other's interpretations of religion, politics, and science were. That is why taking on a topic like this is so interesting to me. Now I would have to try to present and explain these questions to my classmates when I didn't understand them myself.

As I began to brainstorm for my paper, I chose to go outside and gaze up at the sky. Looking up to the snow-capped mountains and breathing fresh air into my nostrils. I thought about how dominant the human eye is to allow us to be able to see all of those things. I pondered the greatness of a higher power and if it existed. Looking up at the clouds and the sun, I thought, *have they always existed?* Looking down at my hands and fingertips and the prints upon them, I wondered, *How is it that from the beginning of the creation of mankind until this present day, each person's fingerprints remain unique to only that individual?*

Like most, I had never given it a second thought. But this time, it sank in. Then I wondered if anyone could count the number of hairs on their head? It would be next to impossible or very tedious, to say the least. Could God or a higher power have already known how many there are? What about the number of stars in the galaxy. Could humanity number those? Could the most powerful of telescopes help us achieve this seemingly impossible task? Also, when you think about the complexity of the human brain, the creator of such an organ must be ingenious. My mind started racing a million miles a minute, hoping that I could remember to write down all these thoughts in my head. Suddenly I heard a voice; it was like a calm whisper and it said, "Both science and God are important to humanity. Without science, there would be no research to find cures for disease and sickness, and there would be no study of the heavens and planets. Humanity would never have ventured out to walk on the moon or build the rockets to fly there. This knowledge had to come from somewhere, but many called it pure science. Without God, would there ever have been the creation of humanity or the very earth that he lives on?" If God created humanity, was he also responsible for giving he/she wisdom and knowledge? I couldn't help but feel relief and astonishment all at the same time while wishing I had brought my notebook outside. I wondered if I had been hearing an actual person's voice, seeing that there was a constant stream of traffic passing by while I stood outdoors. *Had this voice been speaking to my heart and mind, giving me this beautiful explanation of both God and science?*

Honestly, the sound was eerily similar to my late grandfather. Then much like the dreams, the voice was gone. I felt weird. Why do I get these tyes of strange encounters? I knew that I couldn't explain this phenomenon, not in a way that would make sense anyway. I just continued to add more facts to my paper so that my professor and classmates would know that I had studied.

After much anticipation, the big day had finally arrived. I was somehow able to recall and write down everything that was spoken to me and findsupporting facts along with Bible references to strengthen my position. I waited patiently. I was the fourth person to present my project, and boy, was I nervous! I remained confident as I headed to the front of the class. Starting out a bit shaky at first, then I felt a calming feeling come over me and I became more focused and confident.

Is there a difference between religion and science?

Have you ever wondered if the planets were created by God, or did the big bang theory play a role? Consider as I did, the earth we live on, and everything in it or that surrounds it. The sun, the moon, and other planets. What about the wind that blows upon your face? What causes the sun to rise in the east and set in the west? Can these things just happen? Or is there a master creator of all these? Can science and religion co-exist? Is there definitive proof of either?

In researching, I asked myself many questions like, why will no one never share the same fingerprints? Or who can number the stars? Why is the brain such a complex organ to understand and why are we only able to access a limited part of it? How many years has the earth been in existence? Who is God and why can't we ever meet him? I am convinced that there is no right or wrong answer to these questions and many of us will draw our own conclusions in life. But it only matters what you believe and feel in your hearts. That will become your truth; and your explanation.

As I presented my paper, I couldn't help but glance over slightly to see my professor's reaction to the introduction and first paragraph; her head remained down as she wrote notes, pausing only briefly to scan for studentresponses. She then gave me a slight smile and continued grading the presentation.

Although there have been many attempts to explain these complex subjects, a book titled *"Finding Darwin's God"*1 was a helpful and insightful look at just how the author tries to bring together God and evolution. I strongly feel that they can co-exist. After further breaking down my theory of both, I had finally finished my presentation.

There was a moment or two of silence followed by a loud applause. *I can't believe I made it*; I thought as I walked across the room to hand in the report to my professor. As the rest of the students began to present their papers and thesis, I took it all in. It was incredible to see how each person viewed this same subject with a different perspective. The debate to prove God verses science would continue for generations to come.

The next week, I was early to class in anticipation of both my grade and to see what notes, if any, were on the back of the paper. This type of feedback accompanied each assignment returned to the student. I received the essay and was thrilled to notice that I had earned an A. I was so excited that I could hardly contain myself. I just keep staring at my paper, and then I flipped it over to read the critique.

"You took two very controversial subjects and infused them together to increase our understanding of both. There was a considerable amount of research and preparation that went into completing this assignment. I would encourage you to expand your research on this subject. Read books by authors who have taken the controversy of religion and science and have made sense of them. I want to recommend a book to you, primarily because of its overwhelming response, dialogue, controversy, and notoriety that it has drawn from millions of people all over the world. Written by Dan Brown, it's called *The Da Vinci Code*2. It is a fantastic read."

During summer break, I took my professor's advice and purchased a copy of the *Da Vinci Code* on CD so that I could listen on the go. I was intrigued by this brilliantly written book. I was so impressed with the surrounding mysteries of the secret society that I, too, believed that high-ranking officials would go to great lengths to protect secrets or hidden mysteries found in the Bible. I still ponder the question, was Christ married?

It was now about a month into summer break, and I was dying to talk to my professor and get her input on the book. I couldn't arrange a meeting with her in class because she was teaching summer courses, so I met her in the library.

"Good afternoon, Professor."

"Afternoon, Charlie. What brings you back to the place that most students are trying to escape? For the summer at least."

"Well, I took your advice and read *The Da Vinci Code.*"

"What did you think about it? Was it as interesting as I said it would be?" My eyes seemed to say it all, as I began to nod my head.

"Absolutely. I didn't want to put it down and could hardly wait until the next day to pick up where I left off."

"That is good; I like to see the different reactions from students after they read it."

"What reaction would that be?"

She snickered and gave a faint grin. I could see that she was hesitant to divulge what her true thoughts were.

Not sure how to react to her after that. "It was an incredible book, brilliantly written and very intriguing. What is your thought on it?" I asked once again. And just like last time she skirted around my question and gave an indirect answer.

"Truth is this book is open to interpretation, for your interpretations. Some of my past students loved it and agreed with everything, and some thought that there wasn't much truth to its content at all. I usually refrain from giving an opinion about the book so that I don't sway a student either way."

As much as I wanted to hear her thoughts on the book, I had to respect her stance. Then all at once, she began to elaborate on life and some of her experiences.

"Charlie, life is short, so you have to make the most of it. I see a little of myself in you. I was always eager to learn and had to question everything. It helped me become free. And that is how I live my life, free. I don't want to be bogged down with titles, such as Christian non-Christian, saint, sinner, religious, non-religious, believer, or atheist. I do believe in being kind to people and treating them with respect. I trust everyone until they give me a reason not to, and I will do all I can to help others succeed."

"Not to interrupt you, but that is exactly how I feel sometimes. But I should ask, do you believe in a higher power or some greater existence?"

"The thought of a higher power that already knows the outcome of everyone's life scares the heck out of me. I like to think that I'm in control of my destiny and I prosper or fail from the wise or not so wise choices that I make in life. I would be foolish not to understand that there is something out there that is greater than humanity. But what? I'm still not sure. Take Nostradamus for instance. He was very insightful, and his name isn't mentioned that much among Christians even though many of his predictions have come to fruition. I just like to keep an open mind in everything I do, read, see and hear. I get inspiration from the beauty of nature. The birds, the way they sing, they are telling you a story. The trees, the wind, and rain, they all sing praises to something. Each plays their part in sustaining our way of life. My hope for you is that you never settle for someone else's point of view, but form opinions of your own. Charlie, you would be surprised to learn that many authors, producers, and filmmakers tap into some greater power, they just express it through characters and scripts. Are you a fan of Stars Wars?"

"Huge fan."

"I bet you would never guess that those films have spiritual contents in them."

"No, never. Wait, seriously?"

She Laughed! "You still have a lot to learn. Explore the world a little this summer. Will you do that for me? There is a reason I choose to meet you in the library."

"And that is?"

"It contains a wealth of knowledge; you just have to venture out and read all you can."

"Thank you; I got my answer and much more." *I guess?* "Well, professor, I will let you go, thanks again for everything."

"Wait, just a minute, Charlie. I have talked a lot about how I view non-religious things, however, I have had my fair share of bible related discussions also. I was given this information from a strong-willed lady after a long religious debate. I think sharing this with you may be helpful down the road. Let me go and make you a copy of some scriptures that I have found to be somewhat controversial, and you can form your opinion from there."

Professor's Bible Notes

ARRIVING AT HOME about twenty minutes later, I was tired and hungry. *So glad that I took the day off from work*. But after all that I heard today, I was also eager to read what was on the paper.

Isaiah 43 records the prophet Isaiah stating3, "Behold I will do a new thing; now it shall spring forth; shall ye not know it?" Matthew 11 records the Apostle Matthew stating.4 "At the time Jesus answered saying, "I thank thee O Father, Lord of heaven and earth, because thou hast hid these things from the wise and the prudent, and hast revealed them unto babes." Mark 10 records the Apostle Mark stating,5 "But to sit on my right hand and my left hand is not mine to give, but it shall be given to them for whom it is prepared."

Revelation 10 records Apostle John stating, 6 "But in the days of the voice of the seventh angel, when he shall begin to sound, the mystery of God should be finished, as he hath declared to his servants the prophets."

Intriguing very intriguing. But it seems that I have heard this before, I just can't remember where right now.

Soon after talking with the professor, I was interested in gaining another point of view. Maybe someone with a 'true ' religious background. After many days of searching, i chose a chrucrh whos denomination was like mine growing up. So I decided to sit in on a Bible class study one evening. As the pastor began to teach interestingly his topic was "And God said let it be, and it was." He was teaching out of Genesis. I now see how different religious people proclaim that God created the heavens and the earth just by speaking them into existence. This sermon, so to speak was also heartfelt and very interesting. As the class ended, I somehow grew bold enough to make my way down to a small gathering around the pastor. It was sheer curiosity that drove me.

"Sir, I was wondering if I could ask you some questions?" "Sure, young man. And what might your name be?" "Charlie." I replied.

"Well hello, Mr. Charlie, and thank you for coming. I don't recall ever seeing you around here before. Do you live nearby?"

"About 10 miles away. I just looked your church up on the internet and chose to come here."

"Well, I'm glad you did. I believe that everything happens for a reason, and you're coming here may not just be by chance. Before I get too carried away, what's your question?"

"First off, I enjoyed the message; I'm kind of on a crusade to find answers to many different things."

"Thank you; I give all credit to my heavenly Father. I believe I can help you if you want some answers to spiritual things, and I will certainly try with others."

"Well pastor, I was encouraged to read *The Da Vinci Code* by one of my professors. I wondered if you thought it was possible for Jesus to have a wife."

"This subject certainly isn't new to the church, and it stirred up a lot of controversies. I can still recall discussing this book because others have had similar questions. During an evening church discussion, a young minister named Redding had a very prolific answer regarding this very topic." He stated, "Why are people so up in arms about that statement? Even if he were married, he would still be fulfilling the will of God also.

God has sanctioned the institution of marriage. Therefore it wouldn't be going against God's word if he were. What makes Christ so great is the fact that he was willing to die to save humanity and bring us back to God. Being married would not take away from what he accomplished. Although, if you believe the Bible we understand that he was tempted like any other man. I personally believe that he might have wanted a wife, but his time on earth would be cut short."

What a great explanation, I thought to myself. "Was that the only question?"

"Yes, Pastor Davis, for now. That helps me immensely."

"You are sure welcome, and just remember that our church doors are open to all. Feel free to come by anytime."

I was overcome with emotions and wanted to show him the paper that my professor gave me but, I felt that I had already overstayed my welcome, so I just left.

On the drive home, I began to wonder about the emphasis that Dan Brown had put on the importance of women in the Bible. In the *Da Vinci Code*, there were many references to how powerful it is for a woman to have the ability to create life and bring children into this world. I felt that many were willing to downplay this important role so that a woman could remain somewhat unimportant or sidelined in the Bible.

That night I began to think about Christ having a wife, and I wondered if it was possible. Certainly, I would have to do more research to satisfy my ongoing curiosity.

Remembering More of the Dream

IT WAS LATE at night, and I was still awake. Tossing and turning, I knew it would be a sleepless night. I was somewhat troubled because I wanted desperately to make sense of my recent discoveries. I immediately thought to myself, *this was all somehow connected. But how? Why would I get dreams about these women whom I have never met? Why is it that their faces are never evident to me? And what is the mystery surrounding them?* I remained in deep thought, recalling sections of *The Da Vinci Code*, and wondering, *Could this be Mary Magdalene?* When I searched the internet for her name, some sites said that Christ appeared to her first after rising from the dead. *Does that make her special?* All at once, I got a weird feeling about who that woman was and whose clothing she may have been holding. Did Christ leave some garments behind after he died? Was the tomb empty? *Could this have been her on the mountain? What? I mean how anyone could understand all of this is beyond me. If I'm right then she then she was holding the blood-stained garments of Christ?* I began to look around as if I expected someone to answer. I thought I had gone mad. (Laughing,) I had to lay back down to process all the thoughts pouring into my mind. Get a grip, I thought. Other links associated with this site hinted to a biblical reference about a lamb that was slain before the foundations of the world. Revelations 137 *Was this scripture referring to her standing over the body of the sheep? The hood over her face could mean that she was hiding from someone?* Were there people after her? I guess some people would cover their face if they were in mourning. Honestly, I wasn't sure that I was prepared for it all. Would people think I was crazy if I shared it with them? An even scarier was the thought was that someone would want to hurt hurt me because of this discovery. I had to conceal this information until I felt it was the right time. Maybe I will receive another dream with an explanation?

"Man, this kind of sucks," I thought. *"Why me?"*

My Troubled Mind

I ALWAYS OVER-analyze things before making decisions. My employer loved me for it. But the rest of the world sometimes viewed me as a person who was indecisive a problem. But dwelling on these dreams day and night were sure to drive me nuts!

When I returned home to Idaho for spring break to see my parents, I still had so much on my mind. It was good to see my brother, sister and the rest of the family. As we prepared for a BBQ dinner, I couldn't wait to get a taste of home cooking. Finally, it was time to eat. We laughed, played games, and reminisced about the good old days.

My mother, who never held back much, wasted no time starting right in.

"Charlie, I bet you're the only student in the dorms with a neat and tidy room," she said. The family began to laugh. "Oh, you know I love to tease you about that sometimes."

"Anyway, thanks for reminding me that I was such a neat freak, Mother. I hated it! And yes, it carried over to college. Everybody else can leave their room dirty, but I found myself always cleaning up. It bugs me, and that's why I don't have roommates at school anymore."

My mother just laughed and said, "I was the same way as a child so don't worry so much. You're going to make someone a good husband one day; just wait and see."

It was these kinds of talks and openness that made me feel close enough to my mother to open up a little about my dreams and recent discoveries. So after dinner, the opportunity presented itself.

"Mom, I've always been able to come to you with most anything right?"

"Yes," she answered. "You know I've always had a keen sense for picking up if something was troubling you kids. Something is weighing heavily on your mind. Tell me, Charlie, what is it?"

"Well, I don't know if I can share this, but…"

"But what, Charlie? It must really be important and weighing on you. I noticed that you were a little quieter than usual at dinner. You usually have some quick comeback remarks when I tease you. Talk to me. What's bothering you? Are you having dating troubles?"

"No, not yet, thankfully. I've had some strange dreams for some odd reason, and I don't know why."

"What kind of dreams? Tell me about them." "Mom, I'm not even sure what to make of them."

"Charlie you're going to have to elaborate."

"It's just been a series of dreams that I've have had over the past year or so. To me, they serve no particular purpose, so I thought. Now I'm starting to think that there is more to them than I had originally thought."

"Like what?"

"Well, at first I didn't pay much attention to them, but then they kept recurring. Now, I believe they pertain to something important. I am tempted to call them spiritual, but I just don't know how they relate to me or anyone in my life. After all, I'm not exactly the religious type."

"Oh, son, what exactly is the religious type? God can use anyone or anything. You just have to be willing to allow him to do so. Jeremiah8 believed that he was too young to carry out a commandment of the Lord, but God told him to 'say not that I am a child,' and sent him out to complete a task."

"I never would have guessed that these kinds of stories were in the Bible."
"Well, you have to pick it up and read it to know." She began to giggle.

Filled with anticipation about what I was going to say next, she could hardly hold her seat. I smiled at her and said, "I see where I get my sense of humor. Well, they started about a year ago with a dream and now there have been a total of five, to be exact. In each dream, women appear, two of them dressed in white. Does that indicate purity or something?"

"Maybe, Charlie?"

"You know how I am with things, mom. Once I start, I have to dive deeper into the meaning of it, and it's become an obsession."

"Yes, I do know this about you. Do you have any clue who these women are?"

"Well," I said hesitantly. "I believe that one of them was Mary Magdalene."

"What, are you serious?"

"Yes, mom. It appears to be her. Of course, that's just a feeling that I have. She was wearing a white robe and she appeared on a mountain, holding clothing that has red stains all over them. The stains could be blood or wine."

"Whose clothing do you think she is holding? It Mary Magdalene?"
"That's the million-dollar question."

My mother, who faithfully read her Bible every day, began searching scriptures. I could only assume that she was hoping to shed some light on all this to help open up my understanding. Then, as if she knew right where to go, she turned to this scripture.

"Well according to John 19, 9 he was pierced in his side at the end the end, so there could have been lots of blood covering his garments. Not to mention he was brutally beaten. Maybe you saw those clothes? But why would Mary Magdalene be holding them?"

"It's a great question, Mom. Not sure I know how to answer that one."

"Oh, I might be older, but I'm still up on current events. I can see where all the talk of Mary and Christ is leading up to. Now, I have heard a lot of talk about *The Da Vinci Code*, and I'm going to assume you have, too? Or perhaps you have even read it? And while I don't believe that he was married to her, it does raise a few interesting questions, especially, now that you saw a woman holding clothing."

"That's not all. I saw what I believe to be a woman seated on a throne, a chair or something. She sat on the left side of a king or someone significant."

"That is intriguing. For argument's sake, if Christ were married to her, then she would be entitled to things that belong to him. She would also be seated next to him in heaven. That may explain the reason why Christ turned down the mother of Zebedee's children when she asked him to grant her sons the right to sit on his right and left side in the kingdom. In the book of Matthew 2010, Christ answered and said. "Ye know not what ye ask. Are ye able to drink of the cup that I shall drink of, and to be baptized with the baptism that I am baptized with? But to sit on my right hand and on my left is not mine to give, but it shall be given to them for whom it is prepared of my Father. So, I guess that one of those seats could be saved for someone as important as a wife."

"Yeah, that would make sense."

"Tell me more about the other dreams?"

"They are still unclear to me." I tried to change the subject, but my mother wanted to hear more.

"Carry on," she said.

"Well, the other dreams were similar to the first, but again I have no clue what they symbolize."

"Well, I can see why this would be weighing heavily on your mind. It appears that they are more than your ordinary dreams. You may want to throw in a little prayer now and then to guide you."

"I will certainly try Mom, I promise."

"I want to show you something. I think an experience that your father and I had many years ago may give a little insight into what you 're experiencing now, especially since the focal point of your dreams seems to be about women."

A few minutes later she entered the room with a picture album. "These pictures are over twenty years old," she said.

"Wow, I remember some of these."

"I showed you, kids, a few times before, but I kept them hidden, especially when you all were little. I didn't want them to get ruined." Handing me a few pictures, she said, "Look at your father and me; we were so young back then."

"Wow, is that Pops? Man, he was sort of buff for an old man! But you look beautiful as always."

"Thanks, but laugh all you want. Your father was quite the catch." "Okay, enough said. Where were these taken?"

"In California. We were at a church revival to pray for all of God's people."

"Was it a bunch of churches that get together or just our church?"

"Yes many different churches, and it didn't matter the denomination-we all decided to meet up. We fasted and prayed for God's people all over the world. It was one of the best spiritual experiences of my life. The most memorable time of all came on the closing day. Someone invited a woman to speak; she was doing missionary work in the area and heard about our meeting. They called her Rose. There was a powerful presence of God around her. I will never forget her message. It was about, Jesus being the second man Adam from glory who wouldn't fail God. She also mentioned that Jesus live a holy and clean life, and that it meant so much to God that he obeyed his every commandment. Rose also explained that Jesus had to receive the Holy Ghost to be able to complete and fulfill the will of his Father, who had sent him. At the conclusion of her message, she said "remember Eve failed God as well." She ended it right there! It was so powerful and moving that I still get chills to this day thinking about that lady."

I was blown away! I just hugged my mom. She was so touched by the recollection of the week long events, tears began to flow.

"it's okay, Mom. I wasn't even there, but hearing you talk about it and looking at the pictures I can feel your passion."

Something resonated with me when I thought about Eve failing God as well. As I thought about these things, I felt chills run down my spine. For my mom to get so worked up about this message, there had to be more to this.

I wanted to say something. But this was her moment, a spiritual recollection. But, I couldn't get my professor's words out of my head. Do we even know if there is a higher power, a God, or Adam and Eve for that matter?

My Continued Education

FOUR YEARS passed so quickly. I had enjoyed my time in New York, but I grew eager to return home to Boise to be closer to my parents I was offered a great position with a company and I was excited to start my new career. I knew in the back of my mind that if I ever wanted to move up in the company, I would need to further my education and earn a master's degree in business. I set my sights on a religious school again, and I chose Northwestern Nazarene University in my home state.

Many of my friends asked why I chose another religious university since I wasn't really into religion. My answer was simple. I loved debating and learning about other's beliefs. In addition these type of schools offer excellent education at a reasonable price.

The Meeting

ABOUT A MONTH into my fall semester of graduate school, I met a young woman named Tina, who would change my life forever. (And later that year I would meet a couple that would have a significant impact on me as well.) I saw her walking one day through the hall. She was a young, beautiful, olive-skinned, five= foot= something beauty, which was perfect because I was barely 5' 10"myself. She passed me, and I immediately gave chase. As I caught up with her, I asked her how to get to my next class. I couldn't help but notice her beautiful green eyes. She was very helpful, but I'm sure that she knew I was interested in getting to know her. I can't explain it, but there was something special about her.

As we talked more, I learned that she was pursuing a degree in social work with an emphasis in social equality for women. Tina grew up just one state over, in Portland, Oregon. Tina said that she wanted to stay close to home so that she could visit her parents during the holidays. She was from a small family and had only one sibling, a brother named, Jared. Her mother was a social worker and her father was a civil rights attorney.

After we began dating, we shared stories and talked a lot about her interests as well. As we got to know more about each other. Tina admitted to being a little spoiled and a daddy's girl. I laughed and thought to myself, *I'm still in college, living on a budget and trying to pay for school myself. I could never give her everything that her parents did.*

Sensing my reaction, she said she was only spoiled growing up.

"Don't worry; I was daddy's only girl growing up. But I'm independent now. I agreed to pay for my books. My parents help me with tuition and dorm room cost. I chose to move out of state to give myself a little space from my parents. I think it was the right decision, especially because I met you."

I admit, for the first time in a long time, I was speechless. Many of our dates were low-budget ones: dollar movies, fast-food restaurants, or the campus cafeteria. Neither of us seemed to care. We just wanted to spend time with each other. I had become more intrigued by her and our similar interests. We spoke about plans for graduation and a possible future together. We did bump heads a little when it came to religious topics. Tina grew up attending church on a regular basis, and much like my mom, she was skilled and knowledgeable when it came to understanding the scriptures. *I guess that saying holds true, you usually to marry women like your mother,* as for me, I tried to explain things through other means, and I cursed like a sailor. This should be interesting, I thought.

Despite the small clashes between us, we never let our discussions define who we were or would become. I also learned why Tina had such a passion for helping others, especially women and children. She grew up watching her mother find shelter for battered women and their families. I guess this is what drives her to push for change and social equality for females. I admired her passion for change; I began to fall in love. Eight months flew by, and I was thinking about asking her to marry me.

Although I felt close to Tina and hoped that one day she would become my wife, for some reason, I held back discussing my dreams. One reason for not telling anyone, other than my mother, is that I was worried that they'd think I was crazy. I didn't understand what the dreams meant entirely, so how could I explain them to someone else?

My proposal came just a short time later and consisted of a treasure hunt, clues, and a walk down memory lane. I gave Tina a map with clues that lead her to the locations where old friends were waiting to give her the next clue. I waited for Tina at our special place. Waiting alongside me were her parents, some close friends, and a hired singer, and of course the wedding rings. As she walked inside, George began singing, 'You Are So Beautiful to Me.'

She shook, cried, and said yes! There was a lot of planning and stressing as we prepared for the wedding. Two months later, I married the woman I had come to know and love so much.

The wedding was a larger than I had anticipated. It turned out, That Tina and I both had tons of friends and family that loved us very much. She looked so beautiful as she walked down the aisle. Tina's dress was incredible! It was white with lace and it sparkled like diamonds. My jewel was walking toward me. I was trying with everything in me to fight back the tears as I stood there with five of my groomsmen dressed in gray tuxedos with turquoise ties and cummerbunds. Her bridesmaids looked stunning as well. Then, reality finally sank in; the special day was finally here, and this beautiful woman would soon be my wife. How did I get so lucky? We exchanged vows as tears flowed from the both of us. *Finally it was time to kiss my bride*, I thought.

We ate, danced, and sang well into the night. She and her father danced to the song, "I Loved Her First," as I danced with my mom.

After the song was over, her father brought her back to me, and I said, "I know it was hard to give her away, but I promise to take care of her." He smiled as tears began to flow.

We didn't want the night to end; it was one of the best days of our lives. We headed off to start our lives together. Our honeymoon would take place Hawaii, thanks to contributions from family and friends. Talk about incredible views! It was a beautiful place and our resort was fantastic. Our hotel over-looked the beautiful ocean and offered every amenity we could ask for. We felt spoiled. We spent the rest of the day exploring this beauty of the island, and then we were off to a luau.

On the second day, while lying on the beach, I used this relaxation time to talk and be open with my wife."Tina?"

"Yes, honey."

"I have something to tell you."

Her lovely green eyes glazed up at me as if I were going to reveal some shocking secret. Her hands shook the same way they did when I proposed.

"What is it?" she asked in a soft, sweet voice.

"Well, um, well," I said as if her nervousness had infected me. "I haven't told you everything about my past."

"What? What exactly do you mean?

"It's not bad, or at least I think so.It's more on a strange level. In fact, I don't understand everything about what I'm going to tell you. Over the last few years, I've had some strange dreams."

"What kind of dreams? Were they about us?" she asked.

I sat up and calmly put my arm around her. "These dreams are very complicated, and I don't even understand the meaning of them in their entirity."

I used this time to get everything off my chest, holding nothing back.

"Amazing," she said. "It must've been killing you inside to have kept this from me."

"I've always been open and honest with you from the start, about everything. You know that, right?"

"I know you have, and I understand your hesitation now. It wouldn't be easy to tell your girlfriend that you have been having dreams about other women." She began to laugh.

"No, seriously, the dreams that you told me about seem to have spiritual meaning, or perhaps they are just dreams."

"Spiritual? You know that I'm not really into the whole religious thing right? Besides, if they are spiritual, I can't figure out why I was chosen to have them. I mean there are millions of religious people in the world that believe in, and worship God or a higher power. If it turns out that these are spiritual dreams, why didn't God pick someone else?"

"Maybe someone up there thinks that you're as special as I do. Charlie, seriously, I feel that these are more than just dreams, especially because they are recurring. I've watched my mother advocate for women's rights for the majority of my life, so I firmly believe that women have helped change the lives of people all over the world. I believe women will have crucial roles in shaping society and changing our world. So these dreams really aren't strange to me. But I guess time will tell us the real meaning of all this."

"Wow, I want to hear more about some of the women who your mother helped. Did you draw inspiration from any of their stories?"

"Sure. One day Charlie, I will tell you everything. We keep adding to our to-do list, that seems to keep growing," she said with a smirk.

Honeymooning in Hawaii here has been so beautiful and relaxing, I thought. Then I asked my wife, "Can we stay here forever?" "Sure," she replied. "Just as soon as we both become wealthy."

At that moment, we realized that our stay in beautiful Hawaii was coming to an end, and soon it would be back to reality for us.

Chance Meeting?

IT WAS NEARING the end of summer break, and we prepared for our last year of college. When I registered for classes, I was put on a waiting list for business law. I signed up for two courses. However after reading the reviews, I wanted Professor Roy Bartlett. He was a retired lawyer and also a professor. Many online students described him as feisty and very detail-oriented. I believed he would be a great teacher. His online profile showed a well-groomed straightforward-looking guy, with thinning gray hair and a perfectly lined mustache. If a picture is worth a thousand words, his picture says that he took his job seriously. I had no idea of the impact that Professor Bartlett would have on my life.

Running late for my law class on the first day isn't the best way to start off the semester. Making matters worse, the only seat left was right in the front. In a loud voice, the professor stood before the class and reviewed coursework and upcoming assignments. He firmly proclaimed, "You need to come early and pay attention. Those who don't, will probably fail. I don't repeat what I have gone over. So, if you miss it or don't understand a lesson, you will need to come see me after class." (Ah, my suspicions of how he would be were confirmed.)

As luck would have it, my workload increased at work as heavy at my company It was the end of our fiscal year, and everyone seemed anxious to get everything ready for the new year. I started to fall behind with my school work as the semester begun. One day after class I approached Professor Bartlett. It seemed as if all the other students had questions as well. As I waited and noticed another line forming, so I made my way over to that one. At one point, Professor Bartlett stood up and announced that his wife, Claire, would be sitting in on some of his discussions and could help answer questions that students had. I began to make my way over to Claire's line.

Finally, it was my turn. As soon as I saw her, I got this inexplicable feeling that I already knew her. Little did I know, she would significantly impact my life. She was dressed conservatively with a modest up do hairstyle. Her glasses were barely clinging to the tip of her nose. She was wearing a distinct, yet a delightful smelling perfume. I stepped closer before asking her a few questions. To my surprise, she knew a lot about what her husband taught and helped me get caught up on missing assignments. Looking behind me, I noticed that I was the last person in line. I wanted to know a little more about her, so I asked what her occupation was.

"I'm a retired math teacher and a mother of four children, with six grandchildren." She further described herself as a devoted church member and a long-time pianist. *I always loved the piano*, I thought to myself. *Maybe this would be a good opportunity to take lessons from her? But where would I possibly find the time?*

I was also taking another math class. So I solicited help from Mrs. Bartlett and asked if she would be willing to tutor me in math. Mrs. Bartlett laughed and said, "I mention that I was retired, didn't I?" We both laughed, and she stated that she would be more than happy to help with math.

"How much would you charge?"

"Nothing she replied. I'll do it because I've love teaching students math. It gives me joy to help out."

"Thank you so much!" *Thank goodness, I could sure use the help with my math class.*

She continued.

"I prefer to tutor out of my home if that's OK with you?"

"Absolutely," I replied. We exchanged information, and a week later I met up with her and had my first session.

After several visits, I was invited to have dinner with the Bartletts.

I tried to decline, but she insisted. I texted Tina and told her that I would be home later than usual.

When I sat down at the table, I noticed a wall full of family photos. As we ate, I had the chance to ask Mrs. Bartlett about her kids. She replied, "All four live in different states. We miss them and our grandchildren very much."

During dinner, we discussed a lot of topics and then the dreaded question. "Charlie, do you attend church?"

"Not really, I haven't for years. I should warn you, I'm not a very religious person. Although, I will admit that there was something unique or different about the way you prayed and blessed the food. It reminded me of my mother."

"Thank you, young man, that's quite a compliment. I have a faith and belief in God. It sounds like your mother is very spiritual person."

"Boy, is she ever," I replied.

"Well, what happened to you?" She asked.

"I just like to do my own thing, I guess." *Great, another woman in my life that wants to talk religion. Is there no escape?* I thought.

As the weeks passed, it was apparent that I wasn't going to be able to avoid discussions about religion. Mrs. Barlett was a sweet lady, and she explained things so clearly that it was hard for me to be offended by these discussions. Years ago I would have argued and I would have spoken some harsh remarks about religion, or found an excuse not to return to her home. But after these strange dreams, I was seeking answers. I didn't know if she had answers, but it didn't hurt to ask. While eating dinner, I felt more and more comfortable with her; So I proceeded to ask her a question.

"Claire, what are the similarities between Adam and Christ? And why is Christ referred to as the second-man-Adam?" I referenced Rose's message, her message sparked some religious questions, and that was all I was interested in at the moment. My mom was so shaken up about this message, and there was that looming question about Eve. I hope that Claire could provide answers, and later I would somehow find a way to explain the dreams. Mr. Bartlett finished his last bite of dinner and quickly said, "Well, that's my cue to head out. I've had more than my share of religious conversations, and you two seem to be leading up to a major one. I'll let you both finish this and thanks for a great dinner honey." He smiled, excused himself, and limped away.

Claire responded, "Wow, this is an interesting subject. I am somewhat knowledge about why Christ is known as the second man Adam. It's kind of late, and I will need some time to think about it. I'll tell you what. In addition to everything that you have to do for school, I challenge you to do a little research on this subject. I'll do some as well. Next week, we're going to visit the kids and grandkids for the holidays. But in two weeks, when we resume the tutoring we'll compare notes."

I thanked her for dinner and headed home. Over the next two weeks, Tina and I celebrated the holiday with family, and I enlisted her help with the challenging research that Claire had proposed I do over the break.

The Results

HE NEW YEAR had arrived, and this meant that our holiday break was over. I thought, *it's cold, and all I want to do is stay home, sit by the fireplace with my wife, and snuggle.* As I began to relax, I realized today was my tutoring session with Mrs. Bartlett and the analysis of our research would be conducted. I nudged Tina and asked her to accompany me. Tina gave me a look of disparity and said, "Do you know how cold it is out there?"

"Of course I do, silly. But curious about what Claire may have found regarding the research, and I had my session, I just couldn't miss today." Tina carefully gathered her things, and we were off.

When we arrived at the Bartlett's, and I introduced my wife to the couple, and we all sat down. Claire was very friendly. She offered my wife some hot chocolate and a chair by the warm fireplace while, we reviewed my schoolwork. We had a shorter session because I was returning from school break. My professors were trying to ease everyone back into the studying habit. When we finished tutoring, Claire asked us to stay for dinner. How could we refuse? She made homemade chicken soup with some of the best cornbread we'd ever tasted. After we'd eaten, Claire began to clean off the table as if she were in a hurry to get somewhere. She shooed off the professor, who grabbed the crinkled newspaper and slowly moved toward his favorite chair in the living room. Claire ran to the kitchen and came back, beckoning us to follow. Tina and I shrugged our shoulders, looked at each other and gave chase. As we proceeded into the office, Claire spoke. "I found a lot of great information that I want to share with you. But first, to answer the question that you posed a few weeks ago, Charlie, this is what I found. Christ is referred to as the second man Adam from glory that would not fail? The Apostle Paul stated in 1 Corinthians 15^{11} that "The first man Adam was made a living soul; the last man Adam, was made a quickening spirit. So, essentially it's saying that Adam, because of sin, was made mortal. But the second man Adam (Jesus), after his death would become immortal. Since Adam broke the law, man's redemption plan to return to the grace of God would include great suffering and sacrifice. I was shocked to see the similarities between what Adam did to place us in sin and curse humanity, and what had to be done for Christ to redeem us from sin and remove the curse."

Tina could hardly contain herself and chimed in with or research. "I will call this similarity 'the single decision.' Adam chose to eat from the tree that he was commanded not to eat from. That decision affected all humanity, from generation to generation. Sadly, humanity would become acquainted with sadness of losing loved ones, sorrow, and pain because of this decision. Likewise, Christ's decision would affect humanity, this time in a positive way. Although humanity must still face death, we now have the hope of gaining eternal life through Jesus Christ. Also eternal life can be experienced by that quickening spirit which you read about earlier."

"I would never have seen it that way, Tina," Claire responded. Now Claire was up next.

"Digging a little deeper, I looked at the creation of Adam and the birth of Christ. We knew that Adam was not born, but rather formed from the dust of the earth, and created by the mighty hand of God. Well, so was Christ God used the seed of David, preserving it until the right time before placing it in the womb of the virgin, Mary. This can be found in 2 Sam 7^{12}. Both were made of human flesh." Apostle Paul also writes in Corinthians 15^{13}, "All flesh is not the same flesh; but there is one kind of flesh of men, another of beasts, another of fishes, and another of birds. It's puzzling how humanity wants to make Christ a spirit but they are willing to accept Adam as being human even though he was created from the dust, rather than being born. People make Christ different because of the life he lived. We forget he was born of a woman, whereas Adam had no mother or father, but was created by the hand of God. Shouldn't Adam then be referred to as a spirit, a god, or something equally mysterious or significant? Even God refers to him as a man.

It's easy for us to see Adam as human because of his failure, where Christ is viewed as mysterious because of his calling. It appears that humanity easily identifies with failure rather than success? I think our brains are programmed this way. We believe that making mistakes is a part of being human. Because Christ lived a holy life, we try to equate that with being a god, or a spirit.

Tina and I were astonished by her research. "Wow, that's incredible, you were very thorough," Tina said.

"Thank you," Claire said and continued. "However, getting better acquainted with the Adam/Christ comparison gave me insight into just what made Christ so great. Most non-believers will admit that they have some knowledge of Christ. He was human, and although he could have failed God, he chose not to. He realized that Adam failed God and all of humanity, Christ ensured that this didn't happen again."

"He sounds like a nice person, I guess?" I remarked.

"Absolutely, Charlie, he was," she replied, as she once again took the floor. "While conducting my researching, I concluded that the failure was not

entirely Adam's fault." Tina and I looked at each other as if she had just spoken to us in a foreign language.

"What do you mean? Didn't he eat the fruit from the tree which he was commanded not to eat?" Tina yelled, gingerly. It was as if she felt like Claire was going to blame everything on Eve, and the feminist in in her stood up. But then she calmed herself. "Yes, he did," she responded.

"But there is another factor. The flesh of humanity wars against the very presence of God. There is something about it that instinctively wants to oppose God's commandments and do its own thing. Don't misunderstand me; nothing that God creates should be considered flawed. But when humanity was given free will, something in Adam and Eve wanted to obey an object the will of God at the same time. Therefore, when he and Eve were tempted, they utterly failed.

"It is evident to me why God needed Christ to be an example of how humanity should obey him. Christ needed his Father's spirit to dwell in him in order to complete this task. This is the missing ingredient; man needs God's spirit. Because of Christ, God would now understand just why everything else that he created obeyed him except humanity."

Adam failed, and therefore Jesus had to experience everything that humanity would have to go through, as a result of their failure.

Out of all her explanation, I only heard free will. *Yes! Now we're getting somewhere*, I thought to myself.

We do have a free will, just like my professor from New York told me. Now I was starting to side with her a little more, although I had to admit that this Adam vs. Christ thing was interesting. As the conversation progressed, the doorbell rang. Claire answered the door and returned a few minutes later with a lady. She was wearing a long coat and a scarf long enough to wrap around her about three times. When Claire took her coat, I noticed that she was dressed in church attire and wielding a Bible in her hand.

"Oh man, another religious person, and a woman at that. I'm starting to feel outnumbered; I said under my breath." (Or so I thought.) Tina kindly pinched me under my arm and said. "Don't be rude!"

"What?" I said with a grin. *I imagined I look a lot like the Grinch who stole Christmas.* "It's just that I feel bombarded by all of this. That's all."

"I know you do, but we still can't be mean, and this was your idea, remember?"

"I hope you all don't mind," said Claire. "I was researching this subject during the school break and called Maryann to ask her some questions. She began to offer a little insight as we talked, so I asked her to write down some things and meet with us today. I'm sorry I didn't tell you about her coming over. Honestly, I wasn't sure if she was going to make it."

Tina quickly spoke and said, "It's perfectly okay." It was as if she was going to beat me to the punch before I could say something offensive.

Claire brought her up to speed on what had been discussed and then she eagerly inquired as to what new information her friend had found . Maryann put on her glasses and began to look over some papers that she was holding and then she had the floor.

"So, from what you all have already talked about, it seems like it took Jesus to help God understand mankind."

"What do you mean?" asked Claire.

"Well, even though God is all knowing and powerful, he's a spirit and not flesh and blood. How could God understand what it feels like to be tempted, for he can't be tempted with sin? James 1[14]

"On the other hand, humanity cannot understand why God requires obedience, sacrifice, and holiness. But with the Holy Ghost, humanity will began to understand God better, and what makes him so holy and just why he requires faith from his creation."

"I guess you could look at it as the Holy Ghost bridging the gap between

God and man, replied Claire. "This is the reason I wanted her to join us. She has a clear understanding of the Bible. Tina you're raising your hand as if we're in class. I take it you have something to add?"

"If I can interject, that would mean that Jesus gave God a great perspective on what makes humanity tick right?" Everyone looked around at her, simultaneously nodding, pondering what she just said.

Tina, by force, now had the floor and I handed her the rest of the papers.

"Since Christ was a man, he would've known what it was like to be tempted as a man. But doesn't God need a woman perspective as well?" Each of us looked up at her as if she just found the missing piece to the puzzle. I thought to myself, *that wasn't in our notes. Where did that come from?*

"I'm speechless, but you are correct," said Maryann. "As much as Christ loves us, he was a man, not a woman. He couldn't understand the emotions that women feel. He never experienced childbirth or what that entails."

Claire, visibly distraught, said, "That's true. And in the end, if humanity is to be judged, don't you think that both sides have to be represented fairly? Otherwise, the women of the world would appear to have an excuse for their sins."

There was an awkward silence in the room. And I noticed that Claire still had a strange look on her face as she peered into Tina's eyes. *I wondered if she had said something wrong.* Soon everyone collectively gathered their thoughts.

"Should we proceed?" Claire asked.

"Yes, of course. That's what we came here for," I said. I then looked at Tina and wondered what she would say next.

"We discovered similarities with the law. Since Adam was given the law from God and disobeyed it, this would mean that Christ would have to obey every law that was spoken to him by his Father. For this reason alone, God couldn't change his mind, even when Christ asked him too when praying in the garden of Gethsemane. It has been said that Christ never broke a scripture. Well, this was according to the law of God. Now according to the Pharisees and sadducees Christ, broke many laws. One, law in particular that he was accused of was healing on the Sabbath day. Because he was under the commandment of God when he performed these acts, God's laws were broken. We break God's law when we sin or oppose him. Man's law can't make anyone perfect. It's just like the saying: you can please most of the people some of the time or and half of the people all the time. People still find fault with what Christ did. So, Christ sought only to please God, not humanity. Finally, in Matthew 5, Christ stated[15] that he didn't come to destroy the law but to fulfill it. This means that he honored the laws of Moses however, some of those laws would be changed, in order to bring about perfection."

"Makes a lot of sense," declared Claire. Tina continued.

"Another similarity, I guess we can call the 'Great Failure.' Since the fall or sin of humanity took place in the Garden of Eden, where Adam and Eve ate of the tree and learned of good and evil. Another great act would also take place in a garden, the Garden of Gethsemane. While in this garden, Christ asked his disciples to sit and watch with him while he prayed to the Father. He said, in Matthew 26[16] "O my Father, if it be possible, let this cup pass from me." As you read on, you know that Jesus got the victory in this garden. The significance of this prayer is that he made up his mind to die for the redemption of humanity."

"All right," said Claire. "Great job, do we have time for more?" Everyone looked at the clock hanging in the office and smiled. Claire continued, "This next similarity took place after the great sin." Adam was told that "in the sweat of thy face shalt thou eat bread till thou return unto the ground." Genesis 3.[17]

"This meant that humanity would have to work for our food. Jesus himself was not only the son of a carpenter, but he was also a carpenter as well. So he was a partaker of the workforce, no doubt earning a living so that he was able to feed himself. Back to you, Charlie. Do you have anything else?"

"Yes, I said. "I'll call this next one the 'tasting of death.' And the Lord commanded the man in Genesis 2[18] "You are free to eat from any tree in the garden, but you must not eat from the tree of knowledge of good and evil. For when you eat of it, you will surely die." Because of Adams sin, humanity would have to die. For this reason, alone, God couldn't change his mind about Christ going to the cross. He, too, would have to taste death, but he would eventually defeat death."

"OK, that's a perfect point," said Maryann. "Christ had to die. And like a sinner, might I add." She now had the floor.

"This may be more of an irony rather than a similarity. I wasn't as prepared as the three of you, but this seemed to stand out to me. The writer Moses of Genesis 3 states[19], "Thorns also and thistles shall it bring forth thee; and thou shalt eat the herb of the field.' It is symbolic that a crown of thorns was placed upon the head of Christ. Even more ironic is the fact that Christ was given vinegar to drink while on the cross, according to Psalms 69[20]. While conducting research, I learned that vinegar could be used to kill thistle, a thorny flower. Makes you wonder what the symbolism is for the crown of thorns. It may just be a fulfillment of the scripture. Hopefully. I'm not getting off subject too much. What I thought was even more ironic, is that Adam chose to eat from the tree of knowledge when told he would die, but he would not eat from the tree of life, where humanity would gain eternal life. I concluded that Adam and Eve were already immortal and had no need to eat of that tree. It wasn't until they became mortal that God put them out of the garden before they could eat of the tree of life and live forever. It makes you wonder if Christ had to go past the flaming sword that guarded the Garden of Eden and eat of the tree of life, or he would he eat of another tree in heaven to become immortal? "

"So intriguing," said Claire.

"I have one more paper to read, and then we can start to wrap things up." I looked at Tina as if to say will this session ever end? Claire proceeded.

"Now the Bible doesn't tell us exactly what happened to Adam and Eve after their deaths. However, we have enough information about Christ's death and his visit to the underworld-hell-to know that humanity was going to spend eternity there as lost souls. I am thinking about the promise that God made to Christ. Luke the writer of Acts states in the second chapter[21] "Because thou wilt not leave my soul in hell, neither wilt thou suffer thine Holy One to see corruption." My pastor conducted two separate Bible classes explaining the meaning of this scripture. He stated that Christ visited hell like many who had passed on before him. Referring to the scripture in Acts, if God had promised Christ that he wouldn't leave his soul in hell that meant that he was going to visit there but not remain. One church member asked about the promise made to the thief who was being crucified with him that day, and how Christ promised him that he would be with him in paradise. How did Christ go hell and paradise? The pastor responded and said, "Who's to say that he didn't visit paradise first, leave the man's soul there and then descended to fulfill God's word?" He elaborated by saying that "paradise could be a state of mind, where peaceful thoughts occur until Christ returns for us, and then we are taken to our heavenly home. All that was required from the thief to be in paradise was to believe in Christ and the words that he spoke." One of the other church members said this about Christ. "He loved us so much that even at the point of his death, he forgot about his agony to save a thief who believed in him." The Apostle Peter wrote in Peter 4[22] "For this cause was the gospel preached to them who are dead, that they might be judged according to men in the flesh, but live according to God in the spirit." Therefore Christ had to visit hell to preach to those who died before him so that they would be given an opportunity to believe and receive his holy word. And finally, it should be noted that Adam was considered cursed after breaking God's commandment. Well, according to Mosaic Law, anyone who was crucified was also considered cursed. But through his death and resurrection, the curse was removed, as written in Galatians 323 "Christ hath redeemed us from the curse of the law, being made a curse for us; for it is written, Cursed is every one that hangeth on a tree."

"Is that everyone's comparative notes for the evening? This was an amazing experience tonight. I feel that our research has enlightened each of us. May we continue to grow and explore. Thank you all for coming," Claire concluded.

Maryann was the first to leave, and as Tina and I gathered our things. Claire motioned for us to sit tight and then disappeared. Just a few minutes later she came back and handed us a tin. Tina and I tried to decline the gift politely, but Claire insisted that the warm cookies would hold us over until we got home. As I scraped the ice from the car windows, Tina could hardly wait to tear into those wonderful smelling cookies. When we opened the tin, we found a letter from Claire. Tina poked her head out and urged me to finish up so that I could read the letter. Once I had finished and settled into the car, we opened the note and read it out loud. Claire thanked us for coming to her home and told us that the our research was excellent. Toward the end of the letter she urged us to meet again to discuss something in greater detail-something she had worried about discussing with just anyone. We puzzled as to what exactly she wanted to discuss. A little nervous—but excited—we drove off into the night.

The Day After

IT WAS THE day after the big discussion, and my head was still reeling from all that we read. I sat on the couch and stared off into space space. My wife sat beside me and asked what was on my mind. I replied "I'm still thinking about the discussion last night. The discussion was pretty deep, and, to be honest with you, some of it, wait, a lot of it went over my head, even though I helped with the research."

"I know, honey, we may have gotten carried away, but trust me when I tell you that the Bible is full of revelations and mysteries."

"I'll have to take your word for it. I just don't understand everything."
"Like what?"

"Well, for instance, you talked about Adam placing us in sin, but why do we all have to pay for his sins? Why do our loved ones have to die, just because one man decided to eat from some forbidden tree? Why does Adam represent all humanity? Why are there so many people starving to death and then we have billionaires? From the beginning, according to different books and some stories found in the Bible, there were kings and the servants/slaves and masters.

"Why? And why are innocent children and adults killed each day for when they have done nothing to deserve it? Look at all the wars that take tons of lives, not to mention all the horrific shootings of late that destroys lives. I mean, what kind of God or a higher power would will sit back and let that happen?

"Look at the drug epidemic and diseases, like cancer that kills thousands of people each year. I'm just confused, I guess."

"Wow, breathe Charlie! I don't pretend to know all the answers because sometimes I have questions myself. This is how I see things, and this is just my opinion. God gave Adam the law, and he broke it causing humanity to suffer death. God was also so gracious to give us eternal life through Christ. So even if you do die in Christ, you will live again and see your loved ones. A lot of your questions center around free agency. If you think about it, free agency isn't just for the saints of God or people who believe in him; it's for everyone. God wants you to serve him, but with your free will, he won't ever force you to serve him. As a result of this, free agency applies to all people, even those who chose to do evil. They have the freedom to choose wrong, and a lot of them do. Sometimes they hurt our loved ones and even little children. God can protect you from these people, and who knows how many times he has and we never knew about it. He sends angels to watch over us; I know that seems hard to believe. Another unfortunate consequence of Adam's and Eve's transgression is that humanity can now die from diseases like cancer, diabetes, and others. The day they ate of that fruit, humanity would have to die. We spend so much time blaming God, but the truth is the law was given to Adam and then Eve. They should be blamed.

I recall your professor talking to you a few years ago. She believed that we could control our destinies, right?"

"Yes, that's basically what she stated."

"I believe that, too, but only to a certain extent."

"Thank you for that," I replied. "You proved my point exactly-thus making my professor's theories more credible."

"Wait! Just give me a minute to explain. As I mentioned earlier, I believe God sees, and knows all, but will allow life to happen. If he controlled everything, we would simply be puppets and not real people. Here's another example; we, as a media-driven society, tend to highlight all the negative things that take place. Rarely do we focus on the positive outcomes even within a tragedy.

"You mentioned all the shootings at schools and various places. Yes, people have died, but who can explain how guns suddenly jam or an off- duty officer happens to be right on the scene? So, it is still God's grace that helps us through. Take one of the worst attacks on America, 9-11. Unfortunately, people died but how many thousands of lives were spared that day? Those planes traveling at such high rates of speed should have knocked down both buildings instantly, but they stood. Yes, some of it was due to excellent structural engineering, but realistically there was a higher power at work. Not to mention all the first responders whom I call earthly angels who played a huge part in saving lives. As you hear stories from people who were trapped inside the buildings, stating that they heard a voice telling them which stairwell to use, and others recounting their alarms not working so they were late for work.

"Sometimes you have to consider the bigger picture. Yes, God allows bad things to happen to good people, only because people are willing to do these things. This is the part of our destiny that we can control. What we do, how we act, how we treat others, and what we do to others is left up to us to decide. I'm glad that I believe God and his son have prepared a wonderful place for those who choose good instead of evil. When we get to heaven, we will not have to worry about bad people hurting our families, or us anymore."

"Tina, you have a way of calming me. You remind me of my mother, the way you take the time to explain things. I understand what you mean about controlling what we can control and not worrying about the rest. I guess if we knew about the harm that surrounds us every day, we would probably never leave the house."

The Scare

HE WEEK FLEW by and it was Wednesday again. Tina and I speculated and pondered all week long as to what Claire would have to say at our next meeting As soon as we could, we bundled up and headed out to the Bartlett's home. The snow had fallen heavily, earlier that morning but seemed to taper off as the evening progressed. We drove our Durango in case it started snowing again. Traffic was slow and steady. When we arrived, Claire greeted us with a hug. The display of affection caught us off-guard, a little. By now she felt very comfortable with us. As usual, there was a tutoring session for school followed by an invite for Tina to come into the study. Claire offered an apology for not preparing a meal, as usual, stating that she'd not felt up to cooking and had chosen leftovers instead.

"I assume you read my note?" she said.

"Yes, Claire we did," I replied, and Tina nodded.

"Here it is. I wanted to give you both this special gift. It's something that I've been working on for years." Our eyes focused on the box labeled "Claire's Project." She opened it and continued. "I started this quite a while ago but I've never been able to put all the pieces together to write a book."

I looked at Tina as if to ask, *What the heck am I going to do with an unfinished book?* Claire caught the sour expression on my face. I had another h-word in mind but I refrained.

"I know this seems crazy, but I hope that you'll consider it. As you read it, my prayer is that you'll get a better understanding of what I'm trying to say. What I'm giving you is years of hard work, research, and effort that went into these writings. It was written from my heart. I believe that you're the ones that I'm supposed to pass these papers on to. I wasn't sure until I heard Tina ask a question about Eve. Her question seemed to tie in to what I've written. I'm older now and all settled in; all I want to do is help people and visit my children and grandchildren. I have no interest in finishing this project, so hopefully, the two of you will make me proud by finishing what I started."

I was honored and now understood the reason for the outward affection upon arrival. We thanked her and headed toward the door. Then all at once, Tina remember that she'd written down two additional questions from the discussion last week.

"Would it be okay if I ask you a few questions regarding last week's discussion?"

"Sure sweetheart, go ahead."

"Is there a possibility that Adam and Eve could have been Jew or Gentiles?

"Well, Tina, the Bible doesn't give us much of an answer until Abraham concerning Jews and Gentiles. That is a very interesting question though, hang on to that and hopefully, one day we will get an answer..."

"Well Claire, we talked about Adam and the curse upon mankind, resulting from his transgression. Do you believe that Eve's role in the fall placed a curse on mankind as well, particularly women?"

"I believe the curse was removed when Christ died on the cross. This act allowed us to go directly to God with our request, and Christ is our mediator."

"Just one more Claire. If Christ was called a second man Adam, isn't it logical to think that God is going to use a woman to represent a second woman Eve?

"Excellent questions Tina. You all have made my evening. I believe that we stumbled onto something great last week. It's like hidden mysteries were revealed and it makes me wonder if God is still revealing hidden mysteries."

She once again hugged us and opened the door. It was bitterly cold outside, and I noticed that snow had fallen quite a bit during our visit. The Durango was completely covered with snow—so much that I could barely see its dark-blue color. After cleaning it off, we cruised down the streets, switching the vehicle into four-wheel drive. As we were about to turn onto the interstate, the SUV hit a patch of black ice and slid a little bit; this made us both nervous. Tina asked if I was sure I wanted to get onto the freeway.

"It's usually the first place they plow during bad weather," I said, hoping that I was right. "Besides, it'll take twice as long to get home if we don't."

Tina, not wanting to upset me and seeing that I was already anxious, sat back and watched as I white-knuckled the steering wheel and crawled onto the interstate. Looking out for traffic ahead—and Tina saying a prayer—we both noticed that traffic was at a steady but slower-than-usual pace.

After what seemed to be forever, we came upon a highway sign pointing to Center Street exit in two miles. I merged over to the far Right lane so that I could exit on the right. As we began exiting, I noticed a flash of bright lights in the rearview mirror. They seemed to be getting brighter and brighter. I froze; the idiot was traveling too fast for the snowy conditions! With a loud and very hard smash, we were rear-ended by what felt like a freight train. All at once, the Durango slid down the side of the embankment; I could feel the vehicle start to roll, then a white light appeared followed by silence.

Bruised and bleeding from my head, I cleared the contents of the airbag from my face, wiped my eyes, and immediately thought of Tina.

"Tina?" I yelled. "Tina. TINA?" Each cry was more frantic than the last.

With a very faint voice, Tina cried out from a distance, "Honey, I'm all right. I'm okay. How about you?"

"I'm fine. Does anything hurt?" I asked, feeling relieved to know that we were okay.

"My right arm hurts a lot. Other than that, I'm okay."

Just then we heard a voice calling out, "Are you all right?" "Can you get yourself out?"

I reached over and unbuckled my seatbelt. As I looked out the window, I noticed water almost up to my door in all directions. I yelled, "Yes, we can get out. But it look like we're in a pond."

"Stay there for now! I've called 911, and help is on the way."

Out in the distance, I saw a flashlight and once again heard a man calling out, "Are you okay?"

Why would he be asking us again?

I tried to listen as the previous scene replayed itself. "Are you okay? Are you hurt?" There was no response.

Then all at once, I saw the figure of a young man standing over something in the distance, and then he seemed to disappear into the snowy sky.

"Do you see that, honey?" I asked. "What are you talking about?"

"A young boy out there."

"I can't see anything, Charlie."

"Never mind. I think that I'm just seeing things now."

I wiped more blood from my forehead and looked again only to see nothing. I didn't want to sound crazy, so I didn't speak about the figure again. Out of the broken window, we could hear sirens and eventually more voices. "Are you okay?"

"Can you get out of the vehicle?" "I don't think so."

"Hang on—the fire department just arrived, and they'll attend to you shortly."

Tina perked up. "Oh, thank God, help came."

The passenger window and maybe a few others were shattered as well, and freezing air and snow were rushing over her. Just then I remembered. "The box."

"What box?" she said in a stern voice, partially because I had startled her. "The gift box from Mrs. Bartlett!"

I could see her turning around and then groaning in excruciating pain. I peered into the rearview mirror and saw that papers were all over the backseat and the box had taken a beating. *Thank goodness for not only our safety but for keeping the box safe as well. Claire trusted us with her work; I would hate if something happened to it. Plus, if the water were any higher, we would have a soggy mess of paper on our hands.* I thought.

Just then, we heard clamoring as someone yelled, "There is another vehicle that's upside down in this freezing water." Panic and disbelief washed over both of our faces.

Tina cried out, "Did you see another car?" "No," I replied.

"Could it be the car that hit us and caused us to slide off the exit?" she asked. I could see a pale look on her face.

"I don't know."

"Did the person get out?" she asked frantically.

"I sure hope so. I just feel so helpless right now; I wish I could get out and help."

"I know you do, Charlie. But if you do, you'll be stepping into the freezing water and your body temperature will drop like a stone, plus you don't know how badly you could be injured."

"You're right. I hope that help arrives soon to get us out. I'm freezing." I tried to turn over the ignition in the car, but it wouldn't start. We had no power.

Suddenly Tina looked up at me and said, "I don't remember much about the accident. Do you?"

"No," I said. "It's all a blur to me. I recall hearing a loud sound and then seeing a white mist or light appearing and covering the car, but I thought it was snow or lights from the other car."

"Are you serious?" she asked. "I saw it too! It was the one of the most peaceful feelings that I have ever experienced in my entire life."

"I know; it felt as if time stopped or something. Not sure what that was. But its sure weird how both of us saw and felt the same thing," I said.

Suddenly I heard a man's voice yelling and asking us if we were okay. *I know that they are trying to be helpful, but I would sure love it if someone could help get us out of here,* I thought.

"What's strange to me, Tina, is that I didn't see you through the whole experience. I just felt like you were safe and that we would not be harmed."

"I felt the same way. I was a little scared that I couldn't see you. It all happened so fast, yet it felt as if time stopped somehow."

"Either the time stopped, or we were going in slow motion," I said. "I heard the sound of the impact, but didn't see much after that."

"I feel so blessed to be alive," she said.

"Me too, honey. Me too." Time passed, and eventually I felt a hand on my shoulder, shaking me.

"Wake up!"

Did I fall asleep? I wondered. Help had arrived. As the firefighters were pulling us out of the vehicle, I looked in the backseat and thought of the papers once again. I told the rescuers that those documents back there were important and I refuse to leave them in the truck.

Tina looked at me as if I were crazy and said, "After everything we've just endured, you're concerned about those papers. I don't know why you didn't get them before help arrived! Get them, then. I don't have the strength to argue."

I gathered all of the papers and exited the driver's side rear door of the SUV with the help of the firefighters. When we were finally away from the water, we were immediately met with warm blankets and first responders who began treating our injuries and taking our vital signs while inside the ambulance, we saw a police officer walking by. Not able to contain my curiosity, I stopped him and asked about the driver in the other car. The officer told us that the other driver was bad off and most likely wouldn't make it.

"He is being transported to the hospital as we speak. That's all the information that I have for you." Tina and I were dumbstruck. I asked her.

"How did we survive while the other driver likely perished in the same pond? Was it by chance? What kept us from being severely injured? Was it in the plan for the other driver to be fatally injured? If God does exist, why does take a life and leave another behind?" I was left with more questions than answers. It was very unsettling, and once again, my thoughts consume me.

"Sir, you're looking a little faint, and that concerns us," said one of the EMTs on the scene. "Why don't you lie back?" He also said that they would be taking Tina to another ambulance right by me. I agreed and slowly laid my head on the stretcher. Still shaken up by what the officer had explained to us, I wanted it all to just be a dream. Not long after a man approached the ambulance looking distraught. The other responders were placing blankets around him and urging him to seek medical treatment.

He sternly replied, "I have to make sure that these people are all right." He made his way over to the ambulance, and with his lip noticeably quivering, he said, "I'm so glad that you're both alright."

I thanked him, and asked if he was the person who had been calling out to us.

"Yes, it was me. I was on the exit just a little farther up. My car slid into the guardrail. As I got out to survey the damage, I heard the crash. It worried me, so I jumped up quickly to see two vehicles rolling down the embankment. Shortly after, I couldn't see anything because there was a strange light that blinded me. Just as the light was fading, it looked like your vehicle was going to roll again, but suddenly stopped. Then

everything went dark. I grabbed my flashlight, and I ran down to see if I could help. It's amazing that both vehicles didn't land on top of each other."

"What's your name, sir?"

"David. David Simmons," he replied.

He looked to be an older gentleman because of the gray in his eyebrows it could have been ice or snow though. Poor guy his cheeks were as red as apples; He was shivering because his clothes were soaking wet.

"We are so grateful to you for checking on us. Do you know what happened to the other driver?"

A long pause ensued before he answered, "I don't believe they made it. The car landed upside down, and apparently, the water rushed in the vehicle through the windows, and I do think they were able to get out."

"Do you know if it was a man or woman inside the vehicle?" I asked.

"I'm not sure of that just yet. I tried to flip the car over but it was was just too heavy. I had to get out of the water after trying for a few minutes. I could tell that my body temperature was dropping fast. I felt so helpless; I wanted so badly to help the person trapped in the vehicle."

"I understand that feeling," I said. "You did all that you could. Thanks again for checking on us."

"You folks are lucky."

"We feel so blessed," Tina now rejoining me in my ambulance. She then reached out to comfort me.

"Why was there so much water down there?" I asked.

"Son, there's been a lot of snow lately, and with no place to put it, the plows just send it over the side. When it melts during the day, it creates a small pond. The more it snows and melts, the deeper the water becomes, and we've had a lot of snow lately."

Explaining why the water was there did nothing to calm our nerves.

Tina began sobbing, as she thought about someone losing their life. Strangely enough I just said a prayer for the other person involved in the accident. David's eyes began to form tears, and then he told Tina that it would be okay. He then turned and looked at me.

"What's that you have beside you?"

"Oh, it's a box that was given to us this evening before all of this madness took place."

"It looks like it took a beating."

"Yeah, I was thinking the same thing."

"I guess that's to be expected since it was tossed around a bit. Well, folks, I'm off to get warm before my toes freeze. I can say by looking at both of you that a miracle took place tonight." We agreed and thanked him once again. I was exhausted and told Tina I was going to lye down.

I awoke to doctors putting stitches in the Waking up to doctors putting stitches in the side of my head. I couldn't remember the ride to the hospital. I do remember the doctor asking me about my injuries and suggesting that I get an MRI. I down-played the accident; I just wanted to go home.

After a few hours of having tests performed we finally arrived at home. Still shaken up, we couldn't help but recap the events that unfolded earlier.

"Did you hear what that David guy said to us?" I asked. "Yeah, I did," she replied.

"I'm not sure how much of it I believe or even comprehend. How did our car not land upside down?"

"That's a good question, and what do you think about the bright light that he saw around our truck?" She said.

"I have no clue," I told her.

"Oh, Charlie, that could have been us! We could have been killed tonight." I rushed over to comfort her and held her in my arms.

"I know it's hard to think about what could have happened."

"If David wasn't so convincing, I would have thought that he was nuts, I told her." I wasn't quite sold on the bright light thing. I wanted to call it luck, but the look on his face told me otherwise. I looked up at her, gave a half smile, and just held her.

"I'm wondering if you should have gotten an MRI for your head injury," Tina pointed out.

"Honey, they took a cat scan and didn't find any significant injuries."

"I know, but you hit your head pretty hard; it just worries me." Later that night, as I laid in the bed trying to sleep, I started thinking about the events that had transpired that evening. I looked up at the ceiling in our bedroom and there it was; mist, a bright light or something. I didn't want to wake my sleeping wife, but it felt like some confirmation. It was as if it appeared to assure and perhaps even convince us that, yes, it was there, and, yes, it protected us from death or severe injury that evening. Feeling both illuminated and exhausted, I fell asleep.

The Box

I AWOKE THE next morning to grunts of pain. Tina reached over to check on me.

"Are you all right?" she asked. "I think so."

"Your eye looks like you went a few rounds with a heavyweight fighter," she said with a grin.

"Really?" I got up to survey the damage in the mirror. "Wow. You're right; that's pretty bad. My shoulder and neck hurt a bit as well. How's your arm?"

"Besides being broken? It still hurts, but things could have been worse. We're blessed to be here."

"I don't know what I would have done if I would have lost you last night," I said.

Tina and I teared up as the reality of it all set in. As we collected ourselves, Tina's thoughts quickly turned to the box and papers gifted to us by Claire. Sore, but overcome with anticipation, she stood up and grabbed the box with one hand before returning to where I was sitting.

"Okay, are you ready to see what is inside?" she asked. "I'm not sure I want to."

"Come on; we've been so anxious to see what's in here. Let's do it."

We opened it and began to look over the contents. It appeared to be a manuscript of some sort. Each page was numbered and titled as if Claire had been preparing to publish a book. There were notes, chapters, and even a small table of contents to help organize the work. As we sorted through and separated pages, we lost track of time.

Tina suggested that we call our families to let them know what had happened, and that we were both okay. I called and left a message for my parents, Tina reassure her father that the two of us were safe. It was a small but necessary gesture given our parent's penchant for worry. We returned to sorting the pages. We were up well into the evening before we finished. The completed work resulted in a massive sigh of relief from both of us. Everything appeared to be there. Neither of us could bear the thought of how Claire would've have felt had anything been destroyed in the accident. Setting the papers aside for the evening, we headed to bed. We feel asleep quickly this night; we were exhausted.

I was the first to awaken that morning, and after taking a painkiller, I immediately dove into the stack of papers that were now organized in a huge pile. I divided the stack in half and began to read through the first couple of pages. Halfway through, my phone rang. I was too sore to get up and answer it, so Tina did.

"Hello?"

"Hi Tina, how are you guys? I was so worried about you. Is everything okay?" It was Claire and she was frantic, it could be heard in her voice. She continued. "I got a call from Maryann. She told me about a terrible accident that happened the other night. She thought about it for a day and then decided to call me. The news mentioned the victims' names were Charlie and Tina Cole. She didn't recognize your last name, so she was hesitant to call. Was it you and your husband that were involved in the accident?"

"Yes, Mrs. Bartlett. Unfortunately, it was us. We're doing okay, but I did suffer a broken arm. But it could have been worse. Thank God it wasn't, though."

"Oh, I am so thankful to hear this. I've been feeling so terrible thinking that you left my house and got in an accident. If I had just"

"Claire? Claire! It's okay. It's not your fault. We were hit from behind and slid down an embankment. Nobody could have anticipated that. Besides, the weather was bad, and there are some people who don't slow down for anything."

"I know what you mean; driving scares me nowadays. I can't imagine what you experienced during the accident."

"To be honest with you, there is very little recollection of the crash between us."

"What do you mean?" Claire asked.

"I mean, there were accounts of a white mist/bright light that covered the truck and we can't remember anything after that."

"It sounds like a miracle took place!"

"Well, I'm not going to argue with you on that one. I'm amazed that neither of you were more severely injured."

"Yeah, we feel the same way." There was a brief silence. "Tina?"

"Yes?"

"I hate to bring this up now, especially because you both have been through so much, but was the box lost?" she whispered. "I mean, was it damaged in the accident?"

"It's fine Claire, just a little scattered and out of order, but it appears to be fine."

"I don't mean to sound insensitive, but it's the only copy of the manuscript that I have. I typed it up on an old typewriter years ago, way before saved files and thumb drives existed. I should have made more copies, but I just never got around to it."

"I understand. We will make sure your manuscripts are safe."

"Oh, thank goodness. Thanks for taking care of them. Honestly, things began to get strange from the moment I gave you the box. I don't believe that it was by chance that papers survived the accident. I know that I was supposed to give them to someone. I just wasn't sure to whom until a few weeks ago."

"That was so thoughtful of you, Claire, but I need to ask, why didn't you complete the writings and perhaps create a book?"

"I guess I lacked the faith to finish, and the thought of trying to publish something at my age just wasn't going to happen. (She sighed) I just want to enjoy retirement and visit my children and grandkids. I believe my writings are in the right hands now. I know that both of you will be inspired to not only understand what I have written, but perhaps add to it."

"Thanks, but neither of us consider ourselves to be writers; I'm sure that through divine inspiration, anything is possible."

"Yes, it is. Well, you all take care of yourselves, and I'll talk to you soon."

Tina hung up and turned around about 10 minutes later. She looked exhausted. She explained the reason for the call.

"That was thoughtful of her to check on us." I said.

"Yes, it was. She was also very concerned about the contents in the box. She stated that we have the only manuscript that existed. I'm glad nothing happened to it."

"Me, too," Tina.

She trembled as her eyes filled with tears one last time. I moved up from the floor to gently kiss her on the forehead.

"Enough of the sad stuff. Let's tear into these papers and see what all the fuss is about."

"Sure thing," she said. "Well, I guess there will be no class or work for me today. My arm still hurts, and I just want to take some time off to recover."

I called my job as well, said Tina. We spent the weekend relaxing and reading.

From the Files of Claire Chapter 1

Created In the Image of God

CHAPTER 1 WAS titled "Created in the Image of God." It laid out the groundwork for the book and seemed to define the very intentions of God—and perhaps his plan for humanity. It said that God may have gotten lonely and decided to create man and then woman. I'm not sure about this, but I do know that God has a purpose for our lives. John writes in Revelation 2124, "And I heard a great voice out of the heavens saying, Behold the tabernacle of God is with men, and he will dwell with them, and they shall be his people, and God himself shall be with them, and be their God." Could this be all that God wants for humanity just to dwell in their presence? Mankind would have lived peacefully, and there would have been no sin, death, murders, wars, or hatred among humans. What a world that could have been. According to the book of Revelations, that's how things will be in the end. But look at mankind will endure to return to the very place that God desired for us in the beginning.

The creation of humanity was incredible. Imagine some of God's best artwork, in addition to mankind. Think about the sky, the mountains, the beautiful green and blue oceans, and all places that we call paradise. Once you do this, then you will understand that the creation of humanity was no different. If you were to picture the perfect man or woman, both flawless in appearance, perfect in every aspect, then you would be looking at Adam and Eve. God gave them dominion over all living things, and they were created not to die. Imagine the complexity of a human being, how all the body parts work together to keep us alive God is amazing! At the time of creation, Adam and Eve knew no sin and had no desire for anything other than obeying God's commandment. There was no disease in the human body, and they had no struggles—that is, until they committed the great sin, which plummeted mankind into suffering, disease, and eventually death. For this reason alone, the title of this chapter is so important, as Christ's sufferings would also be immense.

We went on to the second chapter without skipping a beat.

From the Files of Claire Chapter 2

Created in His Image and After His Likeness

CHAPTER 2 WOULD give us a precise definition of exactly whatGod meant when he inspired Moses to write in Genesis 1[25] "Let us make man in our image, after our likeness." The burning question for me is, who was God talking to? God didn't need help making mankind, after all he is the only one who can perform this great task. What God stated seems to have a two-part meaning.

Explaining this will challenge many different theories. The first theory declares that God was speaking to the angels in heaven since they were already created. The second theory suggest that God's word traveled down the line of time, serving as instruction for Christ, and to all others who would be called after Christ to help recreate humanity through a spiritual rebirth in Christ. *Claire had a unique way of breaking down what she defines as "God's intentions."*

Moses also declares in Genesis 1[26] "So God created man in his own image, in the image of God created he; male and female." Webster's dictionary defines an image as the reproduction of the form of a person or object and one that closely resembles its inspiration.[27] The word image can be explained by two different examples. The first example is the definition itself. Since God created male and female in his image, then it must also be said the God, the creator, must have eyes, hands, feet, lips, ears, a nose, and emotions. And while he can take on any form, we have to assume that his image is similar to ours, bearing a strikingly similar physiology.

The Apostle John, the author of the book of John, 1 chapter, states "No

man hath seen God at any time the only begotten Son, which is in the bosom of the Father, he hath declared him." What John is saying here is that God is a spirit, and can't be seen by the human eye. So essentially , his only begotten son, whom he created by his own hands , is close enough to God to declare him to us.

Christ was asked this question by Philip, his disciple , recorded in the book of John 14. [29] "Lord, shew us the Father, and it sufficeth us. Jesus saith unto him, Have I been so long time with you, and yet hast thou not known me, Philip? He that hath seen me hath seen the Father; and how sayest thou then shew us the Father? Believest thou not that I am in the Father, and the Father in me?"

So, is Christ saying that he is the express image of his Father, or in other words he is portraying the visual image or appearance of his Father? And ,is he also be saying if you were to see a visual image of God that it would look just like him? It appears that this is exactly what Christ is saying. This may be uncharted territory, but I had explore and learn more about this topic. Even if Christs image were like that of God's, he would also share visual characteristics of his biological father, David, and his mother, Mary; he would have too.

The next explanation of the word "image," in layman's terms, could be compared to the image of a company, school, airline, etc. Everyone wants to project a positive image . It's vital to the success of a business to maintain a positive image. It can be said that God feels the same way . Since he created mankind in his image , is it God 's desire that they represent him? No one can say with absolute certainty, but it appears that way. If we believe that this is God's desire for humanity, then we must believe that his image was tarnished by the disobedience of Adam and Eve .

Now, humanity would have to show God that a human being, although created differently from the angels, could repair his image but it wouldn't be that simple. It appears that the flesh of humanity was flawed from the beginning and fought against the will of God. It was not until the, emergence of Christ, and his life, death, burial, and resurrection, that the, once tarnished image of God would be restored. And through Christ, God realized that humanity would need something more, the Holy Ghost (his spirit) to ensure that they wouldn't fail when tempted.

According to Webster's dictionary the word *form* is a shape, visual appearance, constitution, or configuration of an object. To associate the concept with what I have already written, we look into the word *form*. This word is included in the definition of the word image. I will begin with what appeared to look like the son of God. According to Daniel, the author of the book of Daniel, chapter 3 states, "He answered and said, Lo, I see four men loose, walking in the midst of the fire, and they have no hurt; and the form of the fourth is like the son of God." We know that three men—Shadrach, Meshach, and Abednego fell bound into the midst of the burning fiery furnace by order of King Nebuchadnezzar of Babylon. When they looked into the flames, they saw four men walking around. Remember, this fire was so hot, it killed the men who placed them into the furnace. I wondered how Nebuchadnezzar knew what the son of man looked like in order to recognize that was him walking around in the fire?

I focused on the fourth, person whose form looked just like the son of God, and why he chose to call it a form instead of saying that it was the son of God with them in the fire. According to the Bible, the son of God had not been born. Many theologians and scholars use this scripture to substantiate their claims that Christ is the eternal God, and that Jesus, who had not yet been born, was in the fire walking around with the three Hebrew men. But that wasn't the case. It said that the *form* looked like the son of God, not that it was the son of God. Everyone's image looks like God's to a certain extent. But Christ's image most resemble God 's image. As I researched the word form a little more, it led me to the word *reproduction*; the word reproduction can be defined as a form of a person or object that closely resembles another . So , Christ was a reproduction of the form of God. This explains why Christ's image and form closely resemble that of his Father. (This seems to correlate and validate the answer that Christ gave to Philip) Also in the case of the three Hebrew men, God showed up in his true form, and this form looked like his son. Another interesting fact is that God chose to come in the form of a man, his son Jesus Christ. After all, he could have just taken theheat out of the fire, and they still would've believed in God because the three men survived the intense heat. But God wanted to show the world that he was with these men.

Before I move on to the word *likeness,* I want to sum up the paragraphs above. We know that Christ was born like any other human being.

People get confused because God, the Father, made Jesus both Lord and Christ. Someone greater than Christ gave him those fantastic titles. God is a spirit and can't be seen. This is the reason why Christ tells us that when we look at him, we see his father. This is because Christ's image looks like that of his heavenly father. Lastly, Christ acknowledges that God is greater than himself, according to Paul and Timothy, co-authors of the book of Philippians. Philippians 2, states, "Who, being in the form of God, thought it not robbery to be equal with God ."[32] Jesus didn't believe that he was taking anything away from God by becoming equal with him-not above him, but equal with him.

Webster defines the word *likeness* as a fact or quality of being alike , resemblance , similarity or equivalence .[33] Now, being in the image of God is one thing because we were created that way. But comparing us to his likeness is quite the tall order because sin crept in . Because of Adams sin, Jesus was chosen to be the perfect example of God's likeness.

In fact, Christ instructed us to be "perfect as your Father in heaven is perfect." in Matthew 5 [34]

As I read this scripture , it scared me to think that I could be like <u>Jesus.</u> However, Christ is instructing us to become perfect like his Father. I studied more about God 's likeness to understand just what Christ was attempting to convey . So , if I become like Christ then I, too , can be counted as being perfect to his Father. Perfection, to God, is simply total obedience and is not to be confused with most people's definition or standards of the word perfection. The apostle John states in John 3 [35] "Beloved, now are we the sons of God and it doth not yet appear what we shall be: but we know that, when he shall appear, we shall be like him; for we shall see him as he is. " So simply stated, humanity must become like Christ—taking on his likeness, being humble, meek, compassionate, forgiving, tolerant, loving and holy. God knew that his son would have a clear understanding of his image and likeness. Essentially, becoming like Christ means you become perfect as his Father in heaven is perfect.

"Claire's insight and biblical interpretations are incredible," Tina said. "With each chapter, I belive we were exploring a deep bibical prophecy." It was more exciting than we could have ever imagined, and the best part was that there was more to come.

The Aftermath

IT HAD BEEN a great start to the morning, but I needed to call the insurance agent and request a rental car. My agent arranged for me toto pick it up. After picking up the vehicle, I went to the police station to get the police report. When I arrived at the station, I learned the the driver of the other vehicle died as a result of the accident. It was noted that he had a blood alcohol level close to two times the legal limit. I stood there in total shock. *All of this because of a drunk driver?* I thought to myself.

My emotions turned from shock to anger. "This idiot could've killed us," I blurted out. The officer understood my anger and stated that this scenario is all too familiar, and the consequences are usually worse for all involved.

I felt a wash of calm come over me I pondered the outcome. The sad thing was because of a careless decision, he paid the ultimate price. I pressed the officer for details about the crash. How fast was he Going? Did he even hit the brakes? How did he die? I immediately regretted these questions. The poor guy hit us at full speed without ever tapping his brakes. Witnesses mentioned they never heard the horn or his brakes skidding, just the crashing of vehicles. If that weren't bad enough, the guy might have been able to save himself had he not been drunk. Then I started to feel bad about letting my emotions get the best of me. I realized that life was lost and there were likely grieving parents and possibly siblings, hurting because of the loss. We've all made bad choices in our lives; it's sad his resulted in death.

I took the report from the officer and walked out of the police station, feeling numb. I got into the rental car, and drove away feeling a little apprehensive about getting on the freeway. *Today I'll take the backroads,*

I thought to myself. As I began cruising along the roadside, some of the events of that night replayed in my head. Why did he do that? Why do people continue to drink and drive? I will never understand the logic behind his decision.

Tina was at home, waiting for me to arrive. I showed her the rental car and tried to remain calm, but she could clearly see that there was something wrong.

"You don't sound too excited."

"Well, I'm happy that the insurance company came through so quickly. However, it was my next stop that didn't go so well."

"Where did you go?"

"I went to the police station to get information about the Durango and to see the police report."

"Did they give you any information?" she asked. "Yes, here it is," I said. Tina reached for it.

"Do I want to read this?"

"Probably not, but go ahead," I said with a sigh.

Tina glanced over the details. "You mean he was drunk?"

"Yeah. According to the report, he was more than two times the legal limit."

"That's horrible." She kept reading and she looked distraught. She sighed when she finished, shaking her head to chase off the memories.

"Look, I can't do this anymore. Let's change the subject; I started making hot chocolate while you were gone. Would you like some?"

"Sure, that always cheers me up. Can you get me some ibuprofen as well? I've been having some weird headaches lately with a little dizziness."

"Charlie, are you feeling okay?" "Yes. I just started feeling this way." "Should we get you to a doctor?"

"I'll be fine. It's nothing that some pills won't take care of," I joked. We sat sipping in silence for a short while. My headache subsided, and then as if we both read each other's minds, our thoughts turned to the manuscripts. I picked it up and began reading chapter 3 to Tina.

From the Files of Claire Chapter 3

God's Continued Plans for His Creation

CHAPTER 3, ACCORDING to Claire, would be a little harder to understand. It stated that in God's creative mind, he had a primaryplan for humanity and a backup plan. As with many great inventors, sometimes you have to try different things. So, I guess God had a plan B that would not fail, in the event plan A did. The creative process begins with a thought. Thoughts are generally written down. An example of this would be for a songwriter (verses), an author (books) and a planner , developer , and an architect (blueprints), and so on. In most cases , the individuals mentioned above have alternate manuscripts , verses, or blue prints just in case plan A fails?

It's a simple concept : first , plan A and then plan B. (Plan A represents Adam and Eve.) Plan B involves Christ and another woman to redeem Eve.) If we are created in the image of God, we have the same thought process . Could it be that we've witnessed the thought process of God ? That he planned and later executed . The difference between God and mankind is that God did not have to write it down ; he simply spoke it into existence. His goal is still the same: he wants humanity to help make man. God's Plan B, consisted of Christ and another woman just in case Adam and Eve failed. Plan B, although a contingency plan, needed to be foolproof and ironclad.

God, who is a spirit knows no sin, knew that plan A would fail, and at one point, God even regretted making humanity, sending the great flood to wipe humans off the face of the earth. The dust of the earth, by which we were created, was inherently flawed. Even when humanity wanted to do the right thing, they struggled. There was a missing component. As time went on, God better understood humanity through righteous men and women. Understanding that the flesh of humanity was enmity to him, God looked into the hearts of humanity and believed that most had good intentions. The flesh of humanity lusts after many things, and every person born of a woman will, at some point, have these problems. This is why Christ, in the book of John 16,36spoke of overcoming the world and the things therein such as the lust of the eye, the lust of the flesh, and the pride of life. Again, these problems plague every human. In order for Plan B to be successful, man would need something to help them. The Holy Ghost, or the Spirit of God is what mankind needs to overcome the temptations found in the world. The Holy Ghost combined with good intentions would become a recipe for success.

Christ showed the world that all things are possible with the Holy Ghost. Christ was subsequently the first to heed to the voice of God in found in Genesis 1[37] which states "Let us make man." He was the first born into the kingdom of God and the first to receive the Holy Ghost. What this means is that he, himself, was made into a new man, and that we must follow in his footsteps. A person must be baptized by submersion to remove adamic sin that everyone is born water in. As you emerge from the water, you are a new man or woman in Jesus. It is a type of rebirth. Thus, we are helping God remake humanity into the creation that he had always intended for us to be. My hypothesis is strengthened with the following scripture referenced by the apostle John in the 3rd chapter.[38] "Jesus answered him and said verily, verily I say unto you except a man be born again, he cannot see or enter the kingdom of God."

Verse four reads[39] "Nicodemus said, unto him, how can a man be born when he is old? Can he enter the second time into his mother's womb, and be born?"

Christ was dealing with a spiritual re-birth (receiving the Holy Ghost) through baptism.

Christ came to this earth over two thousand years ago. However, his instructions are still very clear, for us to help God make mankind. Knowing that God created male and female, women will play a huge role in helping make mankind as well. In summarizing this chapter, God's A and B plan can best be described as God's divine and permissive will. I have heard this argument for most my life; If God knew that humanity was going to fail and he knows the future, then hasn't he has already chosen the path we will take?

I can only explain it as follows: God's divine will for Adam and Eve was for them to obey him and fulfill all his commandments. Had they followed this plan, life would be much different for humanity today. He didn't want us exposed to the knowledge of good and evil. Satan chose evil over good, and look what happened. After the decision to eat of the tree of good and evil, Adam and Eve were now operating in God's permissive will.

Permissive just means 'to permit.' God 'permits' you to do certain things, but there are consequences for choosing this path. We saw this for Adam and Eve, whose consequence ultimately meant death. After Christ came on the scene, he took on the penalties for sin for us, as God, understood why humanity was inclined to make poor decisions.

I'll close this chapter with a few examples of God's divine and permissive will. His divine will for Moses in the book of Numbers 20[40] was for him to speak to the rock. Instead, Moses became angry at the sins of the people, and he smote the rock by throwing it down and breaking it into pieces. Moses had a choice, and he chose to strike the rock rather than speak to it as God commanded. Moses now operating in God's permissive will, unfortunately wasn't able to cross over Jordan and experience the beauty of the promise land that he desired to see. We know that Moses will live in heaven because God loved and forgave him. It's been said that he will appear in the last days.

So as the Bible tells us, Adam was given the law from the mouth of God, and then his wife, Eve, learned of this commandment from her husband.[41] Eve was deceived by the serpent and later brought fruit for Adam to eat from the tree of knowledge of good and evil. It's clear that Adam knew better, but he decided to eat anyway. By making this decision, they altered God's original plan for humanity. There are advantages to obeying his divine will. Adam and Eve didn't want for anything. Their food and shelter was provided for them. In God's permissive will, they had to provide for themselves. But God graciously gave them the free will to choose.

Another example is Christ. He, too, was given instructions concerning God's will for him, and he chose to follow God's divine will. Once he decided to fulfill God's will, he would let nothing stop him. From completing this task. Christ made his choice as a child and from that moment until his dying hour, he did everything according to God's plan. When it was time for Jesus to die, he prayed in the garden to see if God would change his mind and let this cup of death pass. But God wouldn't change his mind. He had to die to save the world.

Tina and I finished on that somber thought.

It was the weekend, and we had a chance to catch up, so we started reading more.

From the Files of Claire Chapter 4

Is This Seat Taken?

THE UNIQUE TITLE alone filled me with excitement. Since my dreams began, I've wondered if anyone knew anything about this. What's so crazy is that a lady that I've only known for a few months contemplated this very question. Really? What are the odds? Tina had a look of astonishment and disbelief.

Anyway, Claire started by saying; that she had always pondered the question, if Christ is seated at the right hand of God, then who might be sitting on the left? Now, this is a different seat or throne than what is described in the book of Mark 10[42] because it is in the very presence of God himself. When Christ was approached on two separate occasions regarding the seats on his right and left side, he gave the definitive answer that it was not his to give. So, we are to conclude that Christ will have his throne with seats on both sides. Even still, how is it that the greatest man to ever live couldn't give these seats away? It says in Matthew 16[43] "And I will give unto thee the keys of the kingdom of heaven." Christ was speaking to the apostle Peter. But he wasn't presenting him with physical keys but instead the knowledge on how to keep the same commandments and teachings that he taught. Christ knew that God was had given him a revelation of who he was. Why wouldn't he offer one of the seats to Peter?

Now, concerning the seat on the left side of his Father, I believe that there's a deeper, hidden symbolism at play here. Since God created both male and female in his image and after his likeness, could this place be given to a woman? It felt like a metaphor for the completion of something. If Christ is his son, this woman would be his daughter? It was crucial for God to reserve this seat. So important in fact, that even Christ wasn't able to offer it to anyone.

As I searched on, I wondered why there weren't any prophecies about this. Perhaps there were but we never either seen or understood. Then it occurred to me about how much controversy there was surrounding the birth of Christ. I'm referring to all the prophets who spoke of Christ before he was even born.

Because of the anticipation surrounding the birth of Christ, King Herod sought to destroy him, sending out a decree that every male child under two years of age should be killed. According to Matthew 2[44] God hid Christ and sheltered him so that neither no hurt nor harm would come to him.

Knowing this, I found it easy to understand why there was no mention of the identity of the woman who will sit on the other seat. I understand that whoever this woman is, she must be special to God.

I had to pause reading for just a minute; I couldn't contain flashbacks to my dreams that I began to have. Again, I couldn't help but wonder if there were others who had had this vision or insight regarding the seat. Most of all, I couldn't believe that I was shown this seat in my dreams and that it was indeed a woman who occupied it.

Tina and I exchanged an excited glance. After a few minutes of an energetic discussion, Tina hit the nail right on the head. "Charlie, you now have some confirmation and/or explanation of your dreams."

"I know," I replied.

Taking a break for breakfast, we headed downstairs. Midway through our meal, the phone rang.

"Charlie, it's for you. It's your mother."

She was calling about the wreck, no doubt. She apologized for not getting back to us sooner. It turns out my parents were out of town for a while. Ever the inquisitive one, she hounded us for every detail about the accident. Toward the end, I think she regretted wanting to know everything, realizing that both of us could've been killed. I shifted the conversation toward something else.

"The amazing thing is, we don't even remember much from the accident. There was some white mist or snow that surrounded our truck; then everything seemed peaceful and quiet, then we came to a stop."

"A white what?" she asked.

"A mist of some sort, like a fog."

"You know they say that when you see that angels are present, don't you?"

"No, I wasn't aware of that. Why would you draw that conclusion? After all, it could have been just fog or snow."

"I can't remember if I told you or not because old people repeat themselves. But when I was first married to your father, we moved into an apartment that apparently had a bad electrical wiring. Of course, we didn't know that. Well, one day I was so anxious to get the laundry done before your father got home from work that I set up the washer and dryer myself. The machine seemed to work fine, but when I went to plug in the dryer, I got the shock of my life. I felt the electricity blast into my fingertips, and my life flashed before my eyes. I saw my childhood, my wedding day, and for some strange reason, three kids. Right after my life played backward and forward I guess, I saw a white mist, and everything slowed down. When it cleared, I was up against the wall, alive but shaken up. When your father got home, he was upset but relieved at the same time. After shutting off the power, he realized that the outlet had been wired wrong. I should have been dead when he got there. I've realized that angels were sent there to watch over me. Not only did I live, but I had three beautiful children. I believe my life was spared for a reason. I feel that all of my children needed to be born and that God was going to have a unique calling for all your lives."

"Mom, I don't know what to say. That story was so amazing, and I don't recall hearing it before, but even if I had, it seems to fit right in with what I experienced. I felt weird, except my life didn't flash before my eyes. Everything was just in slow motion. I now believe that there was something different about what happened to us."

"I'm just so thankful that you both are all right. I love you and will pray for a speedy recovery for you."

After hanging up, I thought about what my mother had said. Maybe my life did have a higher purpose. Could that be why the dreams came to me? Could it also be why the white mist surrounded the car? I explained to Tina how every time I spoke to my mother about something, she turned it spiritual. She shared a story that enlightened my mind and helped my understanding.

I guess it's a gift that she has. I never actually understood it, but now I sort of cherish it.

Finishing up breakfast, we relocated our reading into the living room. Time for chapter 5.

From the Files of Claire Chapter 5

Behind the Veil

CHAPTER 5 WAS called "Behind the Veil." This chapter hinted-at the revealing of heavenly secrets found in the Bible, secrets that we've undoubtedly read before, but we've never understood the real meaning. When most people think of the word "veil," they associate it with an article of clothing worn by a bride at her wedding. The purpose of the veil, in this instance, is to conceal the bride as she walks down the aisle her face and beauty are later revealed husband at the altar. But there's more—much more.

God appeared to Moses several times. The first was in the form of a burning bush. Moses was told to take off his shoes because the ground that he stood on was holy. Moses recalls in the book of Exodus 33[45] "And the Lord spake unto Moses face to face, as a man speaketh unto his friend. And he said thou canst not see my face: for there shall no man see me and live. And it shall come to pass, while in my glory passeth by, that I will put thee in a cliff of rock, and will cover thee with my hand while I pass by. And I will take away my hand, and thou shalt see my back parts: but my face shall not be seen."

I think Moses got a glimpse of the form(s) of God. If he could have seen everything, I firmly believe that one form would have looked like Jesus and the other, a female form. God later met with Moses on Mount Sinai and gave him the Ten Commandments. When Moses went to visit with God, he stayed there for more than forty days. He was in the presence of God because he could not have gone without the necessities like food, water, and shelter. It has been said that a day with God is likened to a thousand years. So, for Moses, he must have felt like it was just a few hours. Also in Exodus 34,[46] after Moses communed with God, his countenance was so bright that he had to "veil" himself. This was done so that he would not scare the people. Even though it's spelled differently, the word veil essentially means to conceal?

In the Bible, the first mention of the word 'veil' is in Genesis 24,[47] where women are found covering themselves. It can also be found in 2 Chronicles 3,[48] where this word is mentioned again in Solomon's Temple. The purpose of this veil was not so much to obscure as it was to shield the most sacred things from the eyes of sinful men. In Solomon's Temple, the veil was placed between the "inner sanctuary" and the "holy of holies."

When Adam and Eve sinned, humanity was cut off from God and had to offer up sacrifices so that he would bless them and continue to lead and guide them. This was no easy task, for the people. During many different periods of time, the people used various types of sacrifices. Now, only the best calves, lambs, or goats were accepted by God. The holy priest would offered up the sacrifices by going into the temple. God required that his people, particularly the priest, be holy and acceptable in his presence. In fact, those who were outside of the temple would tie a bell around the leg of the priest entering in. If they heard the bells ringing, they knew that they were alive. If the ringing stopped, they would start pulling on a rope to remove the dead body from the temple.

Because humanity's sin was so great, God wasn't willing to accept just anything from them. We would have to restore God's love and trust by showing him that there were good people on the earth, and that we wanted to please him and live holy lives.

I discovered a third use of the word 'veil.' It can also mean a person. In other words, a spirit in its truest form can dwell in a person. For example, when God dwelled in Jesus, he was veiled or concealed inside of him. It's

God, but the body acts as a human veil for God. There are many references in the Bible that support this definition where a spirit can't be seen, so it's manifested through someone or something. This was evident when God appeared to Moses in a burning bush. It was God, but Moses in Exodus 3[49] couldn't see him. He saw a burning bush that wasn't consumed. Referring back to an earlier chapter, reusing this scripture is necessary to explain the word veil. Jesus's disciple Philip, asked Jesus, "Lord, shew us the Father and it sufficeth us. In John 14, Jesus said unto him, [50] "Have I been so long time with you, and yet hast thou not known me, Philip? He who has seen me has seen the Father; and how can you say, Show us the Father?" Christ is stating, my Father is dwelling within my vessel. God chose to veil himself through Christ and dwell within him. For God to dwell in someone the person must be a clean, and holy vessel. In John 14, [51] Jesus said, "Believest thou not that I am in the Father, and the Father in me? The words that I speak unto you I speak not of myself, but the Father that dwelleth in me; he doeth the works. Believe me that I am in the Father, and the Father in me: or else believe me for the very work's sake."

Now that I knew God dwelled within Jesus; I found it a little difficult to interpret when God was speaking through Jesus, or when it was Christ himself, speaking. The same can be said about referencing certain scriptures-are they talking about God or Christ? An example of this can be found in John 1.[52] "In the beginning was the Word, and the Word was with God, and the Word was God. The same was in the beginning with God. All things were made by him: and without him was not anything made that was made." Ask God for an understanding of this scripture. By doing so you will realize that Jesus didn't make the world. He was made by God, who created the world, and Adam and Eve. Although Christ was in God's creative mind in the beginning, he had no physical presence on earth or in heaven at that time. As I read on, it gets more confusing. Verse four reads, "In him was life, and the life was the light of man." Verse six, "There was a man sent from God, whose name was John." Verse seven, "The same came for a witness, to bear witness of the Light that all men through him might believe." Interpreting this section, we know that God is the life-giver and that his light was the light that lighteth every man that cometh into the world.

John is sent to bear witness of God first, and then Christ. Verse eleven, "He came unto his own, and his own received him not." This means that he dwelt among the Jews, but they didn't accept God. Verse fourteen switches and now is about Jesus. "And the Word was made flesh and dwelt among us, and we beheld his glory, the glory as of the only begotten of the Father, full of grace and truth."

The bible states "the word was made flesh," The mere fact is that anything that is made has to have a maker. So, not only did God make Jesus, God made Jesus the living word and gave him a quickening spirit. Jesus, being flesh and blood, had become the same word that was in the beginning with God, and was God, and was made flesh. God, dwelt in Jesus, reconciling the world to himself that is why the word was made flesh. (God inside Jesus's fleshly body.) It's confusing, but the key is to remember that God never dwelt in mankind before Christ; so there was no need to make a distinction when God was speaking or Jesus.

As I studied more, I learned that God's spirit dwells with man He does this through the Holy Ghost. God veiled himself in Jesus Christ, once he received the Holy Ghost. God no longer wants to dwell in man-made temples, so he made Jesus his temple. There are many places on earth that we know God, himself visited, but there are only a few where it's been said that he dwelled.

The next dilemma is with the word 'temple.' One describes it as an earthly structure for God to visit. Another definition referred to by Christ can be found in Corinthians 6[53] it reads, "What? Know ye not that your body is the temple of the Holy Ghost, which is in you, which ye have of God, and ye are not your own?" So, Christ was stating that our bodies should and can be a Holy Temple for God's spirit to dwell in. More evidence in John 2.[54] "Jesus answered unto them, Destroy this temple, and in three days I will raise it up." Christ referred to his body as a temple. In 2 Samuel 7, [55]

1–29, David had a desire to build God a temple when he saw that the house that he was living in was a better dwelling place than where the Ark was kept. However, God sent a message through the prophet Nathan, to tell David that because he had shed blood and made war upon the earth, that he couldn't build a house for him. God also expressed his need for a temple in verse six: "From the time I brought the Israelites out of Egypt, I have not lived in a house. I have been moving around all this time with a tent as my home." God promised David that one of his sons would be the next king and that his kingdom would be established forever. He also told David in verse sixteen, "But your family and your kingdom will always continue before me. Your throne will last forever." David trusted God and believed him. In 1 Chronicles 22,[56] David charged his son, Solomon, with the responsibility of building God a temple and gave him instruction on how to complete it. Solomon built God a temple and the Ark of the Covenant was placed therein. Inside the Ark contained a golden jar holding the Manna and Aaron's rod. There was also a veil located farther inside the temple that lead to the holy of holies and the mercy seat. It was said that upon this seat, God himself would dwell and commune with those worthy to enter. This veil, was a constant reminder that man was still not worthy to stand in the presence of God. However, this would soon change.

The final temple was in Jerusalem and is where Jesus was found teaching and preaching the word of God even as a child. Coincidentally, this would be the last brick-and-mortar temple on earth that God would physically dwell in. Since the death, burial, and resurrection of Christ, God had no longer needed to dwell in temples built by man. It is recorded throughout the Bible that every time God leaves these temples, they are eventually destroyed. However, this time God would choose a temple of flesh in which to dwell, his son Jesus. Although Christ was human, if you could have somehow removed the veil, you would have seen God in his truest form. I speculate this is why Christ was so confident when he said in John 2[57] "Destroy this temple, and in three days I will raise it up."

Although God made Christ his dwelling place, he was also gracious enough to allow humanity to partake of his spirit and dwell inside of them. Jesus told his disciples in Acts 1[58] that he would send the comforter to be with them (which is the spirit of God) and to go to the upper room and wait there.

The Dinner

IT HAD BEEN a few weeks since the wreck, and Tina and I were starting to prepare for graduation in a few short months. Our families wanted to get together because of everything we had recently gone through. It was more than just a pre-graduation celebration. It was a testament to our survival. We had survived a life-changing wreck, brush with death, and many exams. We had the scars, a new SUV, and soon a degree to prove it. As the last of the family arrived, Tina nudged me to stand up and welcome everyone.

"Thank you all for coming," I said, as I looked around the table at the restaurant. "We love you all so much and are so glad to have family and friends who supported us through school and this tough year. Being involved in that near-fatal accident makes you look at life differently. We're now more focused on the things that are really important to us, like family and friends. Let us toast to life and living it to the fullest with the ones you love." Cheers rang across the table, and my mom even came over and kissed Tina and me on the cheek. She now had the floor.

"I'm so proud of both of you; graduating will be an amazing accomplishment, and the fact that you got to experience college together makes it even more rewarding. We're so glad that you're both okay."

"Thanks, Mom. And thank all of you for coming out to celebrate with us. Now dig in!"

After dinner, Tina and I were overjoyed with all the hugs and kisses from well-wishers. We saw our guests off one at a time, and toward the end, we were approached by her parents. After some small talk, her dad, Steve, pulled me aside.

"Charlie, come with me for a minute." He quietly ushered me into the hallway.

"Son, I know I don't always show many emotions toward people, but I do want you to know that I'm so proud of you. I never question your ability to love or take care of my daughter, but like any father, I worry about you guys. After the accident, I realized that everything could change at a moment's notice, so you need to tell those you care about just what's on your mind and how you feel about them."

"Thank you, sir."

"It's Steve; we're family. I wanted to give you guys a gift from the wife and me to help with whatever the two of you need." Stretching out his hand, he slipped me an envelope. He offered one final embrace and asked me to open the envelope later that evening. I nodded in agreement, and we returned to our wives.

On the way home, Tina inquired about the conversation between her dad and me.

"So, what did my father say to you?' "Well, he asked me not to say," I joked.

Tina reached over and lightly punched me in the arm. "I'm serious Charlie, was he mean to you?"

"No, love. It was just the exact opposite. He told me that he was proud of us and that the accident made him want to express his feelings more."

"Those words came out of my father's mouth?" "Yes, can you believe it?"

"Not really. I mean, he's always been a great dad. But expressing himself was never a strong characteristic of his. I guess people can change."

"Yeah, it was a great talk, and he also gave me an envelope."

"Open it up," she said. Since I was driving, I handed it to her. Tina anxiously opened the envelope and suddenly fell into a deep silence.

"Charlie, this is a check for ten thousand dollars and two cruise tickets." I swerved. "Are you serious?"

"Yes, honey. It's a cashier's check made out to the both of us." "Unbelievable, Your dad is full of surprises."

"All the excitement has me feeling a little dizzy, Tina." "Charlie, are you feeling ok?"

"Not sure, honey. I'm feeling kind of lightheaded as well."

"Okay, hurry and pull over so that I can drive. I'm starting to worry about you. You've complained about headaches and dizziness for some time, and now this. We need to get you in to see the doctor soon!"

"Not so sure that I want to go back to another hospital after what happened with the accident."

"We need to see if something is going on with you. I'd like you feeling good before we head out on our cruise."

"Okay. I'll make an appointment tomorrow."

As we proceeded down the road, I could feel myself drifting to sleep. I had a plethora of thoughts swirling around in my head; the wonderful dinner that we just had, the gift that was given to us by Tina's parents, my mom's speech, and then the information from Claire. I found myself repeating what I had told Tina earlier that day: "Honey, what are we going to do with the manuscript? Other than just read it to each other?" And then I was out

Vacation

Tina's Recollection: Dear Journal, arriving at the port,

Day one:

ONE VERY LONG month had passed since the dinner, and it was time to leave for the cruise. I need this Mexican Riviera cruise so badly! We've been through so much, now seven days of relaxation. I invited my good friend Sherri to help me unplug and unwind. On the plane ride, I began to pray. I know that I've been inspired, and my mind is going a million miles a minute wondering what Charlie told me that night of our celebration dinner as we drove home. I brought my computer and my trusty notebook/journal to write in. I've been through so much this year; I just need to capture my thoughts on paper.

The first night is just trying to settle in. The welcome show was fantastic; dinner was even better.

Day two:

It was a day out to sea. We sat around, pondering life and sharing stories.

"Sherri, can I ask you a few questions?" "Sure, anything."

"What do you think all of this means? I mean I think there's a purpose for everything that happens to us in life. Right?" Now I felt like my faith was in question and I would now have to heed my own advice.

"Tina, good and bad things happen to everyone. You just should pray and ask God all about it. He'll eventually answer all of your questions in one way or another."

"I guess I'll be on a quest for answers my whole life."

"I suppose so. Join the club," Sherri replied. We both chuckled. Later, back in my cabin, I spent some alone time and again referred

to what Charlie told me, so I began to write. Many events of the past would come and go as I tried hard to recall them, so I wrote in my notebook to keep everything in perspective.

I've experienced a lot this year. Some of it is good and some bad. Earlier, I felt that I'd hit my lowest point, so it was then that I began to pray. The problem with praying is, sometimes I feel like it takes a while to get any answers—or at least have them made plain to me.

Why did this happen to my family, God? That was the one burning question on my mind. I know that he loves us. It's hard to imagine that I am the only one who feels this way. I will have to pray again until I receive some clarity.

"Keep the faith, Tina. I believe that God doesn't give to some and not to others. I'm sure of it." That was the advice that Sherri had given me earlier and it came back to me.

Content with my answer, I decided that I would enjoy God's beautiful artwork and leave my worries behind. There was plenty of time to rejuvenate and relax because seven days can come and go so quickly.

Day 3:

Finally, we reached our first destination. This day promises to be fun filled with exciting adventures. Just like true tourists we shopped and purchased things that I'm sure I will never use. Charlie is going to love hats that I picked out for him. I can't wait to show him what I brought. What do you think Sherri? She chuckled and said, "I believe that we have been shopping for 3 hours. Let's go explore a little more before we have to be back on the boat."

Shopping was great, dinner was even better, looking forward to the next adventure.

Day 4:

Good morning journal; having so much fun, just the break I needed. Headed out to play in the sea.

What a day, who knew that I would be able to snorkel? So much fun! Looking at all the amazing sea creatures swimming all around us, freaked me out.

Honestly; starting to feel a little guilty. Good night. Day 5:

Parasailing? Well maybe, I still haven't worked up enough nerve to do so yet. Everyone is telling me that it will be one of the best experiences of my life. Somehow dangling 50-75 feet in the air over a huge ocean doesn't exactly sound like the time of my life. Here goes nothing.

If there are no more entries, whoever finds this will know that I've died! I guess I shouldn't joke like that. (Smile)

Oh boy, the best day ever!!! Well other than my wedding. Charlie will flip out when I tell him all the details. Now I do not want it to be over. The places that we visited were so beautiful.

Day 6:

A lovely day at sea. Ship entertainment is the best, so much to do so little time. PS: Getting bloated and tired of eating.

Day 7:

Still at sea headed to our port and then home. Those seven days had come and gone so quickly. And to my surprise, I was able to channel a lot of my feelings into my writings. Upon leaving, I was saddened to leave my friend Sherri. She has been my rock and voice of reason this whole cruise. We talked, laughed, and even cried together. But mostly we just enjoyed time away, and sadly we both had to return to our lives. Not feeling up to going home quite yet, I decided to visit with my parents for a couple of days.

Not even a day had passed, and I couldn't help looking at pictures from the cruise, laughing and thinking about all the fun we had. Then I began to pull out old pictures of me growing up and just reminisced about the good times. For some reason, I just wanted to look through my old stuff.

Boy did time go fast! And then I stumbled upon some of my old papers from my first year at college.

It was titled "Influential Women, Past and Present."

Attached were the instructions from my professor, asking us who inspires you to want to make a difference. I just started reading through it.

It read. "Although many men in my life inspired me, like Christ and my Father, to name a few, I chose to write about a few different women who had influenced me to strive for more in my life. Watching my mother deal with battered women and displaced mothers and children, I felt it was important to inspire women to do more, be more. Most of the time these women sacrificed everything to take care of their families, and when the relationship turns bad, they are left with nothing.

I always believed that women were extraordinary. I firmly believed that women were only just now getting the respect and recognition they deserved.

Although I only wrote about a few women, I realized that I had only scratched the surface. There are thousands of women who have done many great things to change the way women are treated today. These women are from all walks of life and play a significant role in promoting spirituality and equality for all individuals. Their diverse backgrounds in religion, politics, entertainment, education, military, and homemaking have helped break through many racial and gender-related barriers, opening doors for other women. Knowing this made me reflect on my experiences and inspired me to go to college.

Influential means 'having the capacity to affect the charter, development, or behavior of someone or something.'[59] I'll start with the very first woman on record, Eve. She was an amazing woman because she was the first to experience womanhood and the first to create life in her womb. Her decision in the garden, however, resulted in women having to experience labor pains. It also affected the charter, development, and behavior of many women for generations to come. As a woman, I'm occasionally reminded of how we were supposed to be the 'weaker' vessel, and how females would never be able to achieve as much, make as much, or hold as high of a position as a man. Thankfully, not every woman bought into the stereotype. And although it still isn't easy for women in today's world, they have managed to achieve beyond anyone's expectations.

Tina's College Essay

Biblical Women

RUTH, FROM THE Bible, was the great-great-grandmother of Christ. She came from humble beginnings. She was from Moab (which is the historical-name for a mountainous strip of land in modern-day Jordan). The land lies alongside much of the eastern shore of the Dead Sea, and people from this region were referred to as Moabites.

Ruth and Orpah were the daughters-in-laws of Naomi, who was an Israelite. What is significant about the story is that the Israelites and Moabites didn't care for one another as people. After Naomi's husband and her two sons had been killed, both women decided to follow Naomi back to Bethlehem. Orpah decided to turn back, but Ruth continued. In the book of Ruth, [60] she gave an amazing speech in which she says, "Where you go, I will go; your people shall be my people and you're God, my God." Ruth later married Boaz, and he often called her "a woman of noble character."[61] Although she came from humble beginnings, she was instrumental in helping move God's plan toward the fulfillment of using the seed of David to bring Christ into the world.

Esther, a young Jewish orphan, was chosen by King Ahasuerus of Persia to be his wife. Esther concealed the fact that she was Jewish. Young Esther had to make a life-changing decision: whether or not to go before the king and plead for not only the life of her cousin Mordecai but for all Jewish people living in the Persian Empire. This happened because Mordecai offended a high court official named Haman, who then decided not only to kill Mordecai but all the Jews. Esther went before the king on two separate occasions to plead for their lives. Esther is best known for the quote, [62] "if

I perish, I perish" Esther found favor with the king, who then turned the tables on Haman and had him hanged on the very gibbet he had built for Mordecai. There were many more wonderful biblical stories to speak of, like of the Virgin Mary and Mary Magdalene, but I have chosen just to highlight these two great women from the Bible.

Humanitarian Women

MOTHER TERESA WAS born in 1910. At an early age, Agnes learned to care and share with others from her mother, Drana, who would extend an invitation to the poor to come and dine with her family.

Later Agnes would feel a religious calling at the age of 12. Then six years later she became a nun and took on the name Sister Mary Teresa. She would travel to many different countries, teaching geography and history and was dedicated to alleviating young girl's poverty through education. Dedicating her life to helping others, she was described as a kind, generous, loving, and committed woman. Sister Mary would soon change her name after taking another vow of poverty, chastity, and obedience. And would be referred to as Mother Teresa.

After receiving what she called "a call within a calling" she would travel many more places, opening homes for the poor, sick, and forgotten. This included the first American-based house of charity in 1971 and The Gift of Love home for people with HIV/AIDS in 1985.

She would go on to receive many accolades and awards for her charitable works, such as the Jewel of India, the Soviet Union's Gold Medal of the Peace Committee, and the Nobel Peace Prize, recognizing her work by bringing help to suffering humanity. Passing away in 1997, she leaves a lasting legacy.[63]

The Television Industry

OPRAH WINFREY, BORN in the early fifties, was a young lady who faced many different obstacles growing up. America was still racially divided. She had to deal with segregation and outright dislike for people of color. Moving to Nashville Tennessee, she attended Tennessee State University in 1971. While there she began a radio and television broadcasting. Oprah later moved to Chicago, where she was offered a chance to host her own morning TV show. It was a move that would soon catapult her to first place in TV ratings. She launched her show in 1986 as a nationally syndicated program, with its placement on more than 120 channels. She would later go on to develop Harpo Productions and would be able to benefit more from its syndication. Being able to relate on so many different levels with women and men all over the world, she became one of the highest-rated talk show hosts that this country had ever seen. Tackling issues that America sometimes wanted to forget about and sweep under the rug, but refusing to give in to the usual trashy commentary that was on other shows she became one of the most respected and relatable women ever to be on television. Her show has given many a platform to speak and has opened many doors for women. Oprah continues to be an incredible presence in the lives of many and has given back to the community considerably, including building a school in Africa for young girls called Oprah Winfrey Leadership Academy for Girls.[64]

Political Personalities

JUDGE LISA HALL has continued to inspire women all over the world. Her rise from the poverty-stricken streets of Brooklyn to become one of the most well-respected judges in America makes her one of a kind. In her book, titled *Speaking to the Heart and Soul of Every Woman*, she writes, "I am going to challenge every woman to remove the word *can't* from their vocabulary. *Can't* is a word that can bind and defeat you. As a woman, you can do anything that you set your mind to."

Judge Lisa recalls her struggles of growing up poor but never allowing her circumstances to overtake her will to succeed. "You don't have to be rich or attend the best schools to be a good student." The book also states that she endured many different struggles, from the temptation of gang involvement to being teased for not having the best clothing. She knew what it was like for children to go through hard times. "Although I am tough on some, it's because I recognize the potential that they have. I also seek other means of corrections or counseling to help the child before settling on incarceration," replied the judge when asked where she stood on corrective action for offenders. Her plans for the future may include a run for Senate or perhaps a chance to become a judge on the nation's highest court, the Supreme Court," she stated.

A Homemaker With a Vision

SANDRA GRAY, A former insurance agency owner and now a stay- at home mother of two, from California, has changed women's lives for the better. Sandra has always had a love for helping people within her business and by making sure they had the right coverage for home and auto. Soon after deciding to stay at home, Sandra still wanted to try and make a difference in people's lives.

Two years later, she partnered with Karen, another stay-at-home mom, and formed a company that helps women from all backgrounds get a fresh start after they have been in abusive relationships. Her company has gained fame and notoriety for the difference that it is making in women's lives and now has eight major sponsors. These sponsors donate a wide array of products like computers, food, clothing, and monetary gifts so that many displaced women and their children can begin new lives. Sandra and Karen have set up transportation and job-training programs that prepare women for the workforce. Sandra once said, "My greatest joys in life, other than having my family, is seeing the joy that this program brings to families in need. I feel like this is more of a calling than a job." Sandra and Karen both received keys to the city and many more accolades for their humanitarian work within the community. They continue to run a successful company.

Conclusion

THESE WOMEN THAT I wrote about have inspired change, some on a smaller scale while others on a much larger. All share one thing in common, belief. They believed that what they were doing could make things easier for their, families, race, communities, and gender. Again, I have only scratched the surface of highlighting women who do and have done incredible things to changes lives. I hope that this shines a light on the fact that although women have made many strides in today's world, there is still a long way to go for total equality. Society as a whole needs to continue progressing by recognizing and rewarding women for their amazing accomplishments. I have recently found out just how strong a woman can be when faced with adversity.

Oh wow, I almost forgot I wrote that, it's been so long ago, so I grabbed this report, and a few other keepsakes and packed them into my luggage. I then visited with my parents and old friends; we just enjoyed each other's company and friendship for a while.

Home Sweet Home

Tina's Recollection:

Dear journal;

ARRIVING HOME WAS bittersweet. I felt so relaxed from the vacation, yet there was so much to process still. The reality of it all was starting to set in. As I walked through the house, it felt so empty, so I went upstairs and called out for Charlie. I opened the closet to start the daunting task of unpacking and hanging up clothes. As I began to put my shoes on the shelf, I noticed a box. It looked a little mangled, and I wondered why we'd kept it around. I reached up and brought it down. Initially, the box looked empty, but there was a sound at the bottom like there was something else in there. I felt around and pushed in the middle of the box, and it gave way. Inside were papers, each labeled as if they were chapters. It felt all too familiar to me, but I couldn't recall why. I stopped what I was doing and began to read. It was labeled chapter 6. I couldn't help but wonder if there were more chapters before this. So, I read on.

The Bride and Bridegroom

THERE HAVE BEEN many references made in the Bible about the "bride and bridegroom." What are these references about? The explanation is profound! Now, let's look at one scripture that will help give us a better understanding. Matthew 25 begins, [65] "Then shall the kingdom of heaven be likened unto ten virgins, which took their lamps and went forth to meet the bridegroom. Five were wise, and five were foolish." The ten virgins represented purity, and their lamps were their vessels. The oil represents the Holy Ghost. Therefore, before the return of Christ, humanity will need to become pure. Purity can be achieved through baptism and receiving the Holy Ghost. The wisdom and understanding that you need to be baptized makes you wise, yet having the Holy Ghost and not living by the principles of the gospel makes you foolish. "While the bridegroom tarried (whom we can safely say is Christ), they all slumbered and slept." Now , this scripture pertains to a spiritual sleep because , obviously humans must sleep.

Now, summarizing the events of this chapter, a cry was made, and the virgins rose to trim their lamps . Those with no oil asked for some , from others ,but their requests were denied . Those with oil only had enough for themselves . I find this scenario disappointing because the Holy Ghost was freely given to these five virgins..

They should have been able to give it to others. The moral of this parable is that none of the virgins were prepared and missed the signs that the bridegroom was going to return. Those who were ready went in with him (Christ) to the marriage Matthew 24, [66] states "Watch, therefore , for ye know not the day nor the hour wherein the son of man cometh."

The next few scriptures will pertained to the title of this chapter and will hopefully provide more insight about the bride and bridegroom . John wrote in Revelations19[67]"For the marriage of the Lamb is come, and his wife hath made herself ready." We know that the woman—more commonly referred to in a wedding ceremony as the bride—represents[68] the church. Revelation 21 reads, "And I John, saw the holy city, new Jerusalem, coming down from God out of heaven, prepared as a bride for her husband adorned for her husband." Revelation 21[69] reads, "Come hither and I will shew thee the bride, the Lamb's wife. And he carried me away in the spirit to a great and high mountain and shewed me that great city, the Holy Jerusalem, descending out of the heaven from God. Having the glory of God; and her light was like unto a stone most precious, even like a jasper stone, clear as crystal." So, this great city coming out of heaven symbolizes not only the bride or church but also a reunion of God's people to his son, the precious Lamb.

In summary, I believe the reason there are so many references to the bride or church is that a woman will come to prepare the church to meet the bridegroom. Because the bridegroom has tarried for more than two thousand years, the saints of God find themselves in a state of sleep and slumbering. I believe this woman will help prepare the saints before the cry is made and before the bridegroom returns to get his bride. The parable of the ten virgins is another warning to the saints of God to be watchful and ever ready for the return of Christ.

As the chapter ended , I felt inspired , and honestly a little confused . I knew very little about this lady, Claire . I wished Charlie were here to help me understand the meaning of all of this. But something inside of me wouldn't allow me to stop reading.

A Second Woman Eve?

HOW IS IT that we have come to understand that God will use a woman? Perhaps, one of the first indicators is the fact that hecreated male and female. The second indicator is the fact that Adam and Eve failed God. Now we turn to other indicators that have a more profound explanation.

The prophet Joel speaks about this topic, in Joel 2, [70] the Lord states, "And it shall come to pass in the last days, I will pour out my spirit upon all flesh, and your sons and daughters shall prophesy ." The second prophet tospeak on this subject was Isaiah. In the book of Isaiah, 43[71] God states, "Behold I will do a new thing." This means that God will do something that has never been done before with mankind. In 2 Corinthians 12, [72] Paul had a heavenly experience . He recalls hearing things that were not lawful to be uttered . Could Paul have heard her name being spoken, or heard something said that pertained to her ? Was there something that Paul heard that shocked him ? Could this be the same thing that John heard in Revelations 10 ? [73]"And when the seven thunders had uttered their voices, I John was about to write. And I heard a voice from heaven saying unto me. Seal up those things which the seven thunders uttered, and write them not. But in the days of the voice of the seventh angel , when he shall begin to sound, the mystery of God should be finished, as he hath declared to his servants the prophets." For those who have said that the mystery of God was finished with the ascension of Christ , or could this scripture be pertaining to someone else?

The word "servant," as it pertains to God, is a good thing. It simply means one who is willing to serve him. This includes pastors, ministers, teachers, or anyone preaching and teaching God's word or anyone who is ready to work for him. Many suggest that you have to stand behind a pulpit , speaking his word to be a servant . Becoming a pastor or leader is certainly a great calling; however, you can serve others by feeding the homeless , visiting the sickevealed , and brokenhearted , or by donating money.

Colossians 1^{74} states, "Even the mystery which hath been hidden from the ages and from the generations but is now made manifest to the saints. To whom God would make known what is the riches of the glory of this mystery among the Gentiles."

So, now we know that there is a mystery that has yet to be revealed to humanity and that God will reveal this mystery to his servants. The last verse of this scripture refers specifically to the Gentiles. Why were the Gentiles only mentioned ? It appears that God, himself, hid this mystery for generations, but is now ready to reveal this mystery to the Gentiles in these latter day. Why doesn't this scripture include the Jews ? The Gentiles , were considered as heathens and weren't worthy of the priesthood or to receive salvation according to Jewish laws. That is why we find Apostle

Paul speaking about Christ moving us from the Le-vet'-ic-al priesthood to the Mel-chis'e-dec priesthood.

In this Epistle , Apostle Paul, describes a high priest, which we under-stand is Jesus. In Hebrews 7^{75} it says "If therefore perfection were by the Le-vit'-ical priesthood (for under it the people received the law,) what further need was there that another priest should rise and not be called after the order of Aaron? For the priesthood being changed, there is made of necessity a change also of the law. For he whom these things are spoken pertaineth to another tribe, of which no man gave attendance at the altar.

For it is evident that our Lord (Jesus) sprang out of Juda, of which tribe Moses spake nothing concerning the priesthood. And it is yet far more evident that after the similitude of Mel-chis'e-dec there ariseth another priest." Hebrews 5[76] states, "So also Christ glorified not himself to be made a high priest." This means that God ordained him a high priest. As he saith also in another place, "Thou art a priest forever after the order of (Mel-chis'edec)."

This may be far out there or closer than we think. Has the door been opened for someone else to become a high priest ? Could this be the mystery that God spoke about? It is important to understand that Christ didn't glorify himself to be made a high priest! This means God ordained him to become a high priest. So, is it very likely, and even possible that God will call another high priest after the order of Melchis'e-dec, but this time a woman. If this is the case, she, like Christ, will have a significant impact on Christianity . Her mission, or God's plan for her, will be to allow him

to dwell in her so that he can once again visit his people, but this his visitation will be to the Gentiles.

She, like Christ, will restore God's image. She will succeed where Eve failed, ultimately pleasing God. In addition to restoring God's image, she will prepare the church (which is commonly referred to as the bride) for the return of Christ. Ironically , women or the mother help prepare the bride for the wedding . If this comes to pass , this scenario wouldn't 't take anything thing away from Christ. The fact that a man, with flesh and blood like every other person born of a woman, gave his life to save ours, only adds to his greatness.

From the Files of Claire Chapter 8

Hidden From the Wise and Prudent

DURING THE WRITING of this chapter I asked myself, "how could this mystery have been hidden from the most knowledgeable bible scholars?" Jesus can be found thanking his father in Matthew 11[77] saying, "O Father, Lord of heaven and earth, because thou hast hid these things from the wise and prudent, and hast revealed them unto babes."

What does it meant to be wise and prudent. Is there anything wrong with being wise? Can a person be too wise? Certainly, everyone want's wisdom so that they can become more successful, or, at least, be able to make better decisions in life.

Becoming wise in every aspect of your life can be a good thing. In fact, this is exactly what God wants us to do. He tells us in James 1,[78] "If any of you lack wisdom, let him ask of God, that giveth to all men liberally , and upbraideth not; and it shall be given him."

So, how is being wise a bad thing? It could be when a person thinks they are too wise to take God's word at face value. The birth of Christ is a perfect example . Many theologians have tried to figure out how this could happen . They even question God's plan for saving his creation . Why is it so strange

that God preserved the seed of David and then placed it into a virgin woman? God later gave mankind the same knowledge . In fact doctor's use this knowledge today and perform a procedure known as artificial insemination.

Some people go as far as to believe that they have figured out God's plan for the last days. It's important to understand the Bible, but we must know that God is so complex that we can never figure out his next move, or when he will send his son back for his people.

King Herod was informed, by the wise men, that a male child would be born, and he would become "King of the Jews." Fearing that his kingdom would be seized, and that he would be replaced as king, he decreed that every male child under the age of two be put to death. The king was wise in his attempt to preserve his kingdom, but the wisdom of God is unmatched. God hid Jesus in Egypt until Herod's death, protecting him from danger until the decree had passed.

Being prudent can be characterized or marked as one with much wisdom or judiciousness.[79] A prudent person can also be defined as an educated, profound, or a high ranked individual. A person of this stature will likely revert to their education and/or experience to try and explain Gods methodology. For the prudent man or woman, taking Gods word at face value may be difficult. From a child's perspective, the world appears so innocent. They are solely reliant upon their parents or caregiver(s) to analyze the world for them, discerning what is both good and bad. As we mature physically and spiritually, God desire's, for us is to remain innocent like children, and pure in heart, especially when it comes to trusting his word. Apostle Matthew in chapter 5[80] states, "Blessed are the pure in heart for they shall see God." In this scripture there is a mystery. In John 1[81] it states, "That no man hath seen God at any time; the only begotten Son, which is in the bosom of the Father, he hath declared him." So is the Apostle Matthew saying that we see God only when we die? Or is there a deeper, Spiritual meaning? In John 14, [82] Jesus tells Philip, "Have I been so long time with you, and yet hast thou not known me, Philip? He that hath seen me hath seen the Father: and howest thou then, Shew us the Father?" Christ is telling Phillip in this scripture that the Father can be seen in him. What Christ is really saying here is that God, the Father, is a spirit and the only way mankind can see him is if her is manifested through someone, and at that time Christ was his chosen vessel. Christ further explains this scripture by stating that mankind will not believe that God is dwelling in him, unless they are pure in heart. Revelations will be revealed in the latter days, in order for us to receive these revelations, from God, through his son, and about his son, Jesus, we must remain humble, and pure in heart.

From the Files of Claire Chapter 9

God's Return to Earth

THIS CHAPTER WILL give more clarification about how and even why God would return to earth John 1 [83] states, "He came to his own, and his own received him not." This verse is referring to the Jewish people. But God will never forsake them because he loved them . Their rejection of God , and his son , ultimately meant that the gospel could now be preached to the Gentiles . According to Acts 11, [84] God intended to save the Gentiles from their sins, and that they too, are his people.

Think of the rejection of Christ from the Jews' perspective they were accustomed to being represented by kings of great stature like Saul , David, and Solomon. These were great kings, whom the people admired. It was prophesied that Jesus would be King of Kings and Lord of Lords. In Revelation 19, [85] the Jews are seeking a king that resembles previous kings, like David, Solomon, and Saul. Christ, who came meek and lowly, and was the son of a carpenter , didn't fit their imagery of a king. What they didn't realize was that greatness ran in his bloodline , and that God promised David that he would raise up a son to sit on his throne forever. Because God was in Jesus , and because Jesus came so meek , and lowly they were rejected by the people that they loved so dearly. Jesus greatness would come through the shedding of his blood, and his resurrection from the grave.

There are a few indicators that God will once again return to earth. First, he tells Jesus in Psalms 110 [86] to sit on his right side while he makes his enemies his footstool. That lets us know God, himself, will take care of them . He didn't give a time -frame ; he just said that he was going to fight this battle for him, so to speak.

This scripture is telling us that God is going to leave the heavens, come down to earth again, and possibly dwell in another vessel in order to make his enemies his footstool. This time would he come in a different form? Perhaps, he will come in the form a woman? (Behold a new thing) If this is the case, will God be rejected again? Sadly, if he manifest himself through a woman, the answer will likely be yes. But God will continue to work to not only make Christ's enemies his footstool, but he will also be preparing his bride (the church) to meet the bridegroom (Jesus). Revelation 19$_{87}$ states, "Let us be glad and rejoice, and give honor to him: for the marriage of the Lamb is come, and his wife (the church) hath made herself ready." It is customary in several countries for women to prepare the bride to meet her groom. Just as God did with Christ, he will use another vessel as his earthly dwelling place, and veil himself using a woman.

Once again this scripture in John 1, [88] will apply. "He came unto his own, and his own received him not. But to as many as received him, to them gave the power to become the sons of God, even to them that believe on his name." This lets us know that there will be people who will accept him just as he appears. Another scripture that coincides with John1 can be found in Revelations 2[89]. "He that hath an ear let him hear what the Spirit saith unto the churches; to him that overcometh will I give to eat of the hidden manna and will give him a white stone and in the stone, a new name written, which no man knoweth saving he that receiveth it."

Why does this scripture refer to a "New Name?" Is this scripture implying that God will, once again, come to earth and this time take on a new name? I believe that this time God will come to the Gentiles, veiled in a woman's body. Through this woman, he will reveal his new name, and deliver a revelation to as many as receive him, through her. He will reveal his identity—but only to those who have an ear to hear what he is saying. Once this mystery is revealed, it will become manna, which is food for the soul to those who receive him.

The last thing I want to mention is that I believe that God has written the name of this woman, whom he will use as an earthly vessel, on this white stone and no man will know this name unless he is meek, humble, and seeks God to receive it.

"I wish there were more," I thought. As I stood over an empty box.

Then my mind began to wonder. **When God returns to earth, and assuming it's a woman he chooses, who is worthy to become the next vessel ? What country will she reside in ? What will be her denomination , religion , or race for that matter ?** I had too many questions and not enough answers.

The Awakening

Tina's Recollection:

IT WAS EARLY on a Sunday morning, and I dressed for church. I followed my routine, the same as I had for the past six months. Head to the hospital to check on Charlie, and then head to church. Standing over his bed, I grabbed Charlie's hand, and I prayed once again for a miracle. This day was different, though. Charlie began to open his eyes and gave me a vague smile. I yelled for the medical staff, and several nurses ran in. Going through protocol, they checked his vital signs, and looked at each other for an explanation. One nurse asked me what happened.

"He opened his eyes and smiled at me!" I said. "Are you sure?" another nurse replied.

"I'm positive! Look up at the monitor; his vitals are slightly improving." I told her.

"Okay, Mrs. Cole. Let's not get too excited. He's shown some great spikes in his vitals before." Not willing to refute what I had seen, I just keep rejoicing.

Suddenly Charlie started to come to. He began looking up at all the tubes that he was connected to and tried pulling them out. The other nurse had to restrain him. He was trying to speak, except he was barely able to talk above a whisper. He pointed to the tube that was down his throat as if he wanted it out. I brought this to the nurse's attention, so she came closer and began asking him questions.

"Hi, Charlie. My name is Mary, and I'm a nurse. I have to let the doctor assess your condition before I can remove anything from you." Her voice sounded thick and muffled even to me so I hoped that he understood. A very long time passed before the doctor arrived.

"Charlie, I'm going to look you over and make sure that you are doing Okay. Do you understand?" A nod of the head was an indication that he understood. The doctor dove into his work, explaining as he went.

"I know that it will be hard for you to talk, so nod if you understand what I'm saying. You've been in a coma for about six months, so we need to check how things are going inside of your body."

A short time later, Charlie's room began to fill up with doctors and specialists from the hospital. One doctor explained to Charlie that he was lucky because this doesn't happen every day. Then he approached me and told me that Charlie was coherent and responding to commands, and that was a good sign.

"We have your husband scheduled for a series of tests over the next few days, Mrs. Cole. We want to make sure that his brain and other parts of his body are functioning normally. While we as doctors believe in the healing powers of medicine, we're never too proud to admit when we're taken by surprise. Some cases like your husbands can baffle even the most skilled and knowledgeable of doctors. Some would say it's a miracle. I don't want you to get your hopes up too fast, he may not mentally be the same person that you knew right away, or ever. He has a long recovery ahead of him, so you will need to help and support him through it all. Judging by your frequent visits, I don't think that will be an issue."

"I will do everything I can to help him get better. I've done a lot of soul searching and praying while he was up here, and I remember getting a strong feeling that my husband would be okay. Sometimes I questioned myself; and wondered if I might be crazy for hoping for a full recovery, but I never lost faith."

Just as I finished speaking, Dr. James stepped into the hallway and motioned for me to follow.

"Can you wait here just a minute? I have something that I'd like to show you."

"Sure I can," I responded. The doctor disappeared into his office and came back holding a big yellow envelope.

"Come sit with me, Mrs. Cole." I rushed over to see just what he was holding.

"I wanted you to see exactly why my staff, colleagues, and I are so amazed. Over the course of six months, Charlie has had some unusual brain spikes, including the very last one, just before waking up. The first, as you recall, pretty much gave us renewed signs of life, and I think made your decision much easier as to keep him here with us."

I couldn't help but start to tear up.

"These spikes are unusually high for a person in a coma. They're more commonly seen in patients who participate in sleep studies who have been experiencing very intense or bad dreams. Each time they wake up, they recall falling out of midair, or being chased by something. It will be unlikely that Charlie remembers anything about his state of mind while he was in the coma, we just don't know."

"Why are you holding so many?"

"Each one of these represents a time he had these incredible spikes, and it happened a total of three times. We're impressed with just one. But this is rare."

The doctor shook my hand and walked away. I just stood there in amazement. Filled with joy and excitement, I rushed into the room. Charlie was still surrounded by the medical staff, again checking him over. Late into the evening, all those tests started coming back with positive results. I just kept thanking God for keeping him safe—and me sane—through this whole ordeal. As family members began to arrive, they all showed up with excitement, overwhelming joy, belief, and some disbelief. But they all knew that a miracle had taken place. Charlie, overwhelmed with all the company crammed into his small hospital room, struggled to remember each of them. He smiled when he saw his dad and two siblings. It was as if he knew them. Charlie's mother then stepped to his side, trying to fight back the tears, kissing him on the cheek, and just hugging him.

"God has given you back to us, and for that, we will be forever grateful. I love you, Charlie," his mother said.

I could see him still struggling to recognize her, but he just kept smiling. And all at once, with a weak voice, it sounded like he said, "I love you, too, Mom."

There wasn't a dry eye in the room after we heard that. The crowd began to thin out , leaving only Charlie and myself . I wanted desperately to know more about what happened to him. He tried to speak again, but his voice was much weaker than it had been earlier in the morning . I stopped him and told him not to try and rush things.

Early that next morning I was there just as Charlie was beginning to wake up.

"How did you sleep last night?" I asked.

"I slept okay." His voice seemed just a little bit stronger today. "I have a question for you, honey." He then directed me to come closer. "I heard many of the staff members talking about how long I was here at the hospital. Has it been six months?"

"Yes, it has been." My response was soft, and I could feel myself starting to choke up. "It's been a very long and scary six months for me and our families." Charlie just stared at me in disbelief.

"Sorry that I put you through all of this," he said.

"You don't need to be sorry for anything. None of this was your fault." "How did I end up in here in the first place?" he asked. "You don't remember?" "No, not really."

I could see that he was struggling to try to remember the even the slightest of details.

"Charlie, don't struggle. The only thing that matters is that you're okay."

A week seemed to come and go so quickly. Charlie continued to receive physical therapy to help him relearn some of his motor functions. I came to visit on a Saturday. Charlie was receiving treatment today. As I walked into the room, I was greeted by a lady.

"Hi, you must be Charlie's wife."

"Yes, I am."

"Hello. My name is Jennifer," she said. She extended her hand out to me and continued, "I'm Charlie's physical therapist. I've been assigned to care for him and watch his progress. My job is to help him get stronger so that he can start walking again on his own. I have to say the Charlie is making good progress and is recovering faster and a lot sooner than we expected."

Both Charlie and I turned and looked at her, feeling so proud and blessed at that moment. It was as if we were reading each other's minds.

Jen continued, "Isn't that right, Charlie? You're ready to get out of here."

"Yes, the sooner, the better. I'm ready to go home," he whispered.

"I know you are. If you keep progressing, it really won't be much longer. We're done with our session for today, so he's all yours."

"Thank you so much for all your help. I know that he has been in good hands."

She excused herself and left us both alone.

I wheeled him down to the cafeteria and ordered lunch. Charlie was now sitting up and feeding himself. He gestured at me to come closer.

"Honey, I am starting to remember some things," he said. "I can remember some accident that we were in. It seems like we were coming home from Claire's house. I remember looking over at you and asking you if you were ok. You told me that your arm was hurting but that other than that, you were fine. How's your arm now? Did I end up here because of the accident."

"It's fine now. But steady, Charlie. Don't get too excited." I leaned in to hug him, and I could feel that his heart was racing. "That's close to how things happened, but not exactly. Let me explain everything to you. We were on the interstate, coming home from your parent's anniversary dinner party. It was snowing a lot as we were heading home. You noticed headlights speeding toward us, and we were struck from behind. Everything seemed to be moving in slow motion; then I woke up in pain. I hurt my arm, and you hit your head fairly hard."

"What about the young guy I saw running across the water, Tina? Don't you remember seeing him?"

"Okay, Charlie. I hate to tell you this, but you were in and out of consciousness after the accident. Lord only knows what all you saw."

"Are you kidding me?" He replied.

"No. I honestly wouldn't joke about something like that. I thought that I had lost you at first. Apparently, as we rolled, you hit your head pretty hard. Your side of the SUV sustained the most damage; we're lucky that you weren't killed. It seemed like we were in the water forever."

"I'm hearing what you're saying, but it still doesn't register. Everything seemed too vivid and real; I could have sworn that I was awake."

"Well, Charlie you were off and on, and we thought everything was just fine. But then…"

"Then what?" He replied. "You fell ill, Charlie."

"That explains a lot, I guess."

As we continued to talk, Charlie just wanted to recap the events from that night. I had been trying to distance myself from even talking about what had happened, but I guessed that this was the only way to heal. We headed back to the room, and Charlie once again brought up that night.

"Tina, are you sure that you don't remember ever seeing a young man run across the water?"

"Charlie, that water was freezing. I doubt that he would have been out there running in the pond. Do you remember reading the police report?"

"No, Tina. Not really. I'm still just remembering bits and pieces now."

"Well, according to the police report a young kid was responsible for driving drunk and hitting us, but he apparently drowned at the scene, still strapped into his vehicle. Not sure if that's the kid you're talking about."

"Oh, no, he died?"

"I'm afraid so." I was starting to feel confused as to how he could remember so many details about the accident. I refrained from saying more and quickly tried to change the subject.

"Charlie, it's okay. You're back here with me now, and everything is going to be fine."

"I can vividly see a box in the backseat. Do you remember anything about that Tina?"

I was trying desperately not to disappoint him. I paused and then said, "There is no box that I know of."

"Really?"

"Honey, you've had a lot of time to dream and think about things.

When you're feeling better, we'll talk more." I was starting to feel overwhelmed, and clearly Charlie was upset, so I decided to grab a soft drink. As I was leaving, I could hear Charlie mumbling, and I could feel his eyes on my back.

My Obsessive Thoughts

TINA HAD TO be crazy! As she walked away, my thoughts started to darken. There was no way that I could accept what she was telling me. Was she deceiving me? Was she playing me for a sucker all this time? Everything seemed so real but mixed up. How could she say that this had never happened? It was true. Wasn't it?

I was now starting to question myself. I just lay there, trying to recall previous events. I couldn't wait until my wife got back because I had to ask another question. I was going to phrase the question differently just in case she was playing games. Then the phone rang. It was Tina; she explained that she was heading home. She felt as if she were upsetting me and that she wanted to get some rest. Two long days passed, and she finally came to visit. "Tina."

"Yes, Charlie."

"I hope that I didn't upset you the other day."

"I'm doing okay, Charlie. It's just that it brought back so many memories, and I thought that I had lost you."

"I understand, honey, and I'm sorry." I still wasn't convinced that she was forthcoming. I wanted to throw a trick question in there.

"I was just wondering how school was going?" I had her now; we'd already graduated.

"Well, it was tough, but I did fine considering the circumstances. It was hard not having you there to help me study, especially with my math homework."

"Math?" I said. "How could I possibly help with math when I needed a tutor myself?"

"You're so silly; math is one of your strongest subjects!"

I paused in shock. I knew that I sometimes performed well in other areas, but certainly not math. "Claire was my tutor. She helped me with my math. How could I need a tutor if I'm so skilled?" Then it hit me like a ton of bricks. The box that was in the back seat belonged to Claire. So, I had to ask again.

"Tina, I just remembered that the box I told you about the other night, it was from Claire."

"Oh, honey. I know that it feels like you've woken up to a different world. But in time, things will start to make sense. They did for me. And to answer your question, I still don't know about this Claire or some box."

What does she mean, they did for her? I thought. Was there something else that she wasn't telling me?

"Charlie, graduation was a great sense of accomplishment. It was all that I thought it would be, having worked so hard for my degree. On the downside, you weren't there, and now you'll have to postpone finishing your degree."

I was hearing my wife talk, but I became disgusted while trying to decipher between what was real and what were figments of my imagination. I remembered facts, but they somehow seemed all jumbled together.

"Charlie, it's going to be okay. You beat the odds when you woke up after so long, and you continue to progress so fast. Regardless if you remember everything, these things are the least of our concerns right now. I'm looking forward to my husband coming home with me again."

As Tina left the hospital for the evening, I began to ask questions of the staff regarding my condition and the accident. Over the next few days, I spoke with doctors and nurses and had them pull charts to get some insight on just what my condition was. I was surprised to learn that I was in and out of consciousness after the accident but had some recollection of the events that had transpired that evening. Somehow, I could remember talking to first responders while being rescued. It appeared that my x-rays didn't give an accurate depiction of what my injuries were. I probably should have received a CT scan that evening. According to doctors, I had developed some significant swelling in the brain. That was why I had been in a coma so long. I was also shocked to learn that apparently, my wife had also sustained a head injury. Naturally concerned, I inquired more about her condition. It turned out that her head trauma hadn't been as severe as mine, but some of the side effects associated with head injuries could be long or short-term memory loss. Sometimes the memory loss can also be brought on by a traumatic event. Maybe what happened to me sent her over the edge? I couldn't help but break down a bit and cry. I felt somewhat responsible because I had been driving. She was such a strong woman. She just didn't want to upset me by telling me everything that she had gone through. All at once, it made sense for her not to remember some things that had taken place before the accident. Suddenly, I didn't feel as crazy.

Another week passed, and finally, it was time to leave the place that I had called home for over nine months. Arriving home felt surreal; I hardly recognized the place. But it felt like home. No more tubes or the sounds of machines beeping. Later that night, even though I should have just been relaxing, I wanted to know more about the accident. The memories and the details were starting to become just too vivid. Tina came and sat down beside me, pulling out a notebook journal.

"What's this?" I asked. "It's my journal."

"I can't recall you ever having one of these before."

"You wouldn't remember, Charlie. I started keeping one after the accident."

"This is something new," I said. All the while I was wondering why she would need one. "Is there something you're not telling me, honey?" I didn't want to reveal what I had learned about her condition after the accident.

"I just wanted to keep a journal of everything now, besides, it gave me something to do while you were in the hospital."

"Can I read it?" I asked. Tina nudged my hand away. "Not right now." I kept staring at the book. "Are all those pages full?"

"Yes. I promise you, Charlie, I will let you see everything, later."

As the week passed by, I became more focused on reading what was in the journal that my wife was keeping from me. As we prepared for bed one night, I opened the dresser drawer, and there it was in plain sight. I quickly grabbed it and opened it. As I began to read page by page, I felt as if I had entered another world or something. There were so many facts and details about our lives, but they seemed backward to me.

Tina's Journal;

Recalling the accident. It was one of the worst days of my life. We were coming home from a pre-graduation celebration party when the crash happened. On a brighter note graduation was terrific! Can't describe the feeling that I got walking across that stage. I felt a sense of accomplishment. There was a noticeable void there though. Charlie!! I'm missing him so much.

I had to pause for a moment, wondering what the facts were. As I remembered it, we had been coming home from Claire's home, yet when

I asked Tina, she had no recollection of Claire. She recalled that we were leaving my parents' anniversary dinner. All these events I was sure it had taken place; I just couldn't remember what order they went. And graduation. Really? I missed out. Saddened by the thought of this, I read on.

I thought that I had lost my husband the day of the accident; I just felt so helpless. Just as I thought things were starting to get back to normal, the unexplainable happened. Charlie developed swelling on the brain. He was exhausted on the car drive home and then went to sleep that night and didn't wake up. I was devastated and felt helpless. I wanted to give up, but I knew that I had to keep living life as usual. I survived off prayers and hope. I knew that I would still have to maintain some normalcy in my life, or I'd lose it. The cruise was a nice distraction, but it wasn't the same without him. My friend was a saint for accompanying me on this much-needed vacation.

I couldn't help but wonder when this cruise took place? The next page read,

For some odd reason, the only thing that seems to soothe my troubled mind is to write and try to stay as busy as possible. I don't understand what all of this means, or why I am going through all of this without him. On a lighter note, I can't wait for Charlie to read my old paper that I found visiting my parents. He used to wonder where I drew some of my inspiration from, well this was a start. Again, missing him so much! So thankful for our families' support. I would've never made it without them. I love staying in touch with Charlie's mom. She is a true saint.

There were more pages detailing trips to the hospital to see me and then nothing for a few weeks.

Hello, journal, I've been so busy with everyday life that I haven't had time to write. I've missed the peace of mind that writing gives me. It felt strange arriving to an empty home. As I began the dauntless task of unpacking, I stumbled upon a beat-up box. As I picked it up to look it over, I heard rattling in the bottom. As I pushed the bottom, it gave way. Taking a closer look, it appeared to be some writings. Each of them was titled. It felt eerie familiar, almost like a déjà vu moment. But with my recent memory troubles I couldn't place it, nor have I ever heard of the lady Claire who appears to be the writer of them. What would we be doing with these strange papers? Oh, well, on my way to the hospital and then to church.

DEAREST JOURNAL;

I have the best news possible; my Charlie woke up today! My prayers have been answered. I wouldn't have believed it myself had I not been standing in the room. What a great and exciting day. A miracle has taken place right in front of my eyes. I've been changed forever.

There were more detailed accounts of me going through the process of regaining my ability to do everything on my own, and this was the entry that changed everything.

Today when I went to see Charlie, he made mention of a box. Could that be the same crumpled box that I discovered up in the closet? Then a short time later he spoke of a Claire and that a box belonged to her. Who is this Claire? Although the pages did have Claire's name at the bottom of them, I can't remember ever meeting her. Why do I feel like I just lied to my best friend, my soulmate? He also said that we read incredible stories from this lady. I can't recall us doing that, either. I honestly didn't want to confuse him any more than he was already, so I played coy. But if Charlie remembers reading stories, it means that there has to be more material, right? All of the pieces should fit

together, but I just don't know how. Perhaps he dreamed all of this? Maybe I did? I'm not sure if we will ever know what is fact or fiction. Good night, journal.

Just then, Tina came out of the bathroom, I hurriedly put the journal away and kissed her good night. I tossed and turned most of the night, apparently waking up my wife. I couldn't contain my thoughts or feelings any longer. As we both lay there half asleep, I had to ask.

"So, honey, when did you write about a box that you found?" Realizing what I was talking about, she reached over and hit me.

"Charlie. I told you that I would let you read it later."

"I know, babe. It was in the dresser drawer, and the temptation was just too great."

"Its fine, Charlie. I just need time to explain everything to you."

I wanted to pick a fight with her so badly! All this time she had information about this Claire lady and the box? But I got a grip on myself and realized that she had been through a lot. It couldn't have been easy watching me lie there not knowing what the outcome will be from day to day. So I changed my thoughts and inquired about her paper she picked up from her parents' house.

"Tell me more about this paper you wrote."

"Everything's up in the closet; you can get it and read it now or in the morning. Either way, I'm headed back to sleep."

"That's fine; I'll read it in the morning. I'm tired too." But I became saddened by the fact that I missed graduation. I just felt like my world had been turned upside down.

Morning came, and after breakfast, Tina went and retrieved the report. I read through what she had written. I felt chills all over my body. She told amazing stories of these women and how they had touched and changed many lives.

"I have to say you wrote amazing things about these women. We talked a little before about this, but it seems like you drew some inspiration from them. Is that why you chose the field of study you did?"

"I've always been interested in learning about the advancements women have made in our society; this was just the first time that I was able to put all my feelings into words. Not to change the subject, but I've been dying to ask you.

"All that time that you were in the coma did you feel like you were dreaming?"

"I'm not sure what you'd call it. It felt like I was dreaming, and then it felt as if I were reliving my childhood. I was able to recall different experiences that I had had over the years with my family."

"I've heard that when you're close to death, your life flashes before your eyes. Maybe yours could have played out in slow motion? Don't you think?"

"It's possible; I still can't believe that I was away from you that long."

"Me neither, I seriously thought that we had lost you." Suddenly, her facial expression changed, "Charlie."

"Yeah."

"I just recalled the doctor showing me the reports regarding your brain activity and a series of spikes. I wonder what those meant."

"I'm not sure why they would have occurred."

Tina, now more intrigued than ever, wanted to know more. She inquired more about what I had dreamed.

"Honestly, other than recalling a few past events, that's about all I have for you."

"Well, Charlie, I have some good news. You'll have some free time here very soon. I'm taking you on a cruise to make up for the vacation that you missed. And did I mention that we're leaving a week from Monday? So, find you flight bags," she said.

"That sounds nice, but don't you remember? I just got back to work."

"Do you think that I would leave out that small detail? Your job has been so supportive through this whole process, and your boss assured me that they would be willing to help in any way possible. Besides, he said that it would be good for us to reconnect. I have to say that you do work for a great company."

"Wow. I guess I do," I replied.

Another Vacation

CHARLIE, YOU HAVE been so focused on that notebook. What have you been writing?"

"I've been trying to recall any small detail that I can remember about being in the hospital."

"Okay, busybody. Save some for the trip. We'll take this time just to relax and talk. We've got a lot of catching up to do. Can you imagine the stories that we'll be able to tell our children?"

"Children. You've never made mention of kids before."

"Well, sweetheart, it's a little bit early, and I didn't want to scare you, but according to a home test, we're having a baby."

"A baby! How? When?" I felt a little embarrassed because I did know how and had an idea of when. We had taken advantage of a few late nights in the hospital as I was recovering.

Overjoyed, I hugged and kissed her. "This is the best news we've had in months. You're making me feel like the most important man in the world right now!"

"You are, to me."

Still, in shock, I held her there in my arms for about five more minutes.

"I don't know what I would have done if I had lost you that night," Tina said. Suddenly, I had a flashback—some recollection of the accident. *I said that very same thing to her after the crash*, I thought to myself. As I continued to stare into space, my face seemed frozen.

"Charlie? Hello, are you okay?"

"Yes. I am." I shook my head to wake myself up.

"The doctor said that you might experience periods of flashbacks or blank stares during the recovery process. It's okay. It just means that your brain is still trying to process everything. He also said that you would try so hard to catch you up on all the things that you've missed, it'll frustrate you at times. I want you just to relax and take things slow."

"I will, honey. I promise."

The week seemed to fly by, and before I knew it we were leaving for vacation. I wanted to get away from everything, relax, and enjoy each other's company.

"Charlie this is the same cruise that I took. But I want you to know that it's even more special this time because it's with you."

"Thanks, sweetie."

Arriving at our destination, the look on Charlie's face was priceless when he seen the size of the cruise ship.

"Charlie, are you ready for seven days of fun?" "Absolutely. But right now, I'm just ready to eat."

"Oh, just you wait, you may get sick of eating toward the end."

"Well, considering that I was tube-fed for six months, I think I will manage." Finally settling into our cabin, I was ready for fun.

Day one:

Out to sea. Sitting on the main deck catching sun rays and relaxing, Tina turned to me and said, "I'll be right back."

"Wait up; I'm coming too."

"Oh, Charlie. You're such a worrywart. I'm just going to the room to get something for you."

As we entered the cabin, Tina reached into her suitcase and handed me a stack of papers.

"What is this, honey?" It appeared to be a bunch of articles. "Whose are they?"

"Sit down, Charlie. I found these at the bottom of a box in our closet when you were in the hospital. But I'm not sure what or who they pertained to. I wanted to tell you, but I honestly didn't want to set your progress back. I knew that you would have become obsessed thinking about them."

As Tina and I both sat on the bed looking over these papers, I noticed titles. Looking at each I felt confused; I had to ask. "If these papers have titles, then they have to be a book, right?" I frantically flipped through each until I reached the last page. There, in black ink, was her name—Claire Bartlett. I gasped and then looked at Tina.

She quickly asked, "Is that the same Claire you had asked about in the hospital?"

"I'm honestly not sure," I replied. "It would have to be, right?" *Everything seems too surreal for me right now.*

"Charlie, hello? Charlie, are you still with me?"

"Yes. Yes, I'm still here. That would mean that she's real. Right?" "There's only one way to find out. Let's go through your cellphone and see if you have her listed as a contact."

I fumbled through my cell phone contacts, and sure enough, there her name was: "Claire Bartlett (tutor)."

"Should I try and call her?" I asked. She was slow to answer, apparently preoccupied with looking over the papers.

As I pressed the buttons, a strange voice came on and said; "Sorry the call you're trying to make did not go through." Silly me; I had forgotten that we were out to sea and headed into international waters now. The anticipation was going to kill us, yet we would have to wait until we docked back in the United States.

My Surrender

Day two: A day at Sea

I WOKE EARLY that morning and attempted to wake my wife, but she wasn't waking up for anything. I got ready for the day and told her I would be on the top deck just relaxing. The ship was just sailing in the open water. As big as this ship was, it felt like a tiny sailboat in these blue waters that seemed to go on forever. Looking out at the sunrise, it somehow harmoniously blended with the sea. As I continued watching, I began to contemplate the creator of such a fantastic sight. Who commanded the sun to rise in the east and set in the west? Did all of this just happen by chance? How is it that the waters are separated from the land? Why are some of the ocean's waters blue, some green and then some not clear at all? I peered up at the blue sky with hints of white clouds and pondered why they seemed so pure. Those same clouds can offer shade from the scorching sun, yet instantly bring rain upon the earth, and some massive storms as well. It was so peaceful and serene on the ship. Everyone seemed equal; you could hardly distinguish between wealthy or middle class.

I was changing inside. I could feel it in my soul. I was seeing the world differently now. Maybe it was all the serenity. Perhaps I was getting worn down. Not to use the obvious ship reference, but I did feel like a battered and worn vessel, one that had been tossed to and fro. I didn't have much fight left in me, it was time to wave the white flag. It's not that I didn't believe in God. There were just so many unexplainable events in the Bible that they almost seemed made up. But I have to say that my recent experiences lead me to believe that not only could some of these stories be true, but there was a real possibility, that there is a God. Waking up after six months was nothing short of a miracle and only added to that theory. There is a possibility that God may have chosen me to deliver a message through these dreams. I guess sometimes you just can't explain the unexplainable! And sometimes events defy explanation. Tina's breakdown of how bad things can happen to good people started to make sense now. I could have died twice within the last year or so. But for some reason, I'm still here. I wouldn't change much about my past, and I'm glad I've taken an objective point of view on things. By doing so, I made my own choice rather to believe in God or not. So many people follow their parent's beliefs, or that of a friend, or other family member, never really knowing for sure in whom or what they believe in. But for me, I gave myself time and a choice. As I sat there in deep thought, I felt a hand on my shoulder.

"Ah, you finally decided to join me." "Yes, Charlie."

"It's pretty late; I was just about to come grab you for breakfast." "How come you don't you ever sleep in?" She asked.

(I winked at her and said) "Just an early riser, I guess."

"Why do I feel like you're teasing me for sleeping in? Apparently, you have forgotten that I'm eating and sleeping for two."

"I understand, honey. It's easy to sleep in, especially when you can sleep so well on the ship. But that internal alarm clock keeps going off in my head pretty early and wakes me up."

"Let's eat. I'm starving!" she urged.

During breakfast, I explained to Tina how I was starting to have a change of heart about spiritual things. Although there was a lot I still didn't understand, I hope with her help I would start to get a better understanding. After we had eaten, we decided to do some research while lying out on the top deck.

The Bible was our first point of reference. I wanted to know about some of the prophets. I knew a little about Nostradamus; now I wanted to know about some of the prophets from the Bible. I always felt like there was a mystery surrounding them. I wanted to see what gave them the spiritual insight that they possessed.

We read for a few hours, and I was amazed. Like Nostradamus, these prophets, spoke about things that have not taken place; very interesting. But then we looked at the papers that Tina brought with her. One paragraph stood out to me: It was about the prophet Joel. He stated in Joel 2,90 "It shall come to pass in that day, afterward, that I will pour my spirit upon all flesh; and your sons and daughters shall prophesy, your old men shall dream dreams, your young men shall see visions."

This gave me a weird feeling. *Could this include me?* I thought. It would make sense. Had I been given some unique insight? Even though they seemed like dreams, were they visions? Could I have been charged with telling the world about my dreams?

Sometimes I think Tina and I are crazy. We seemed to be the only ones who go on vacation to write. However, I felt like I would forget some things if I didn't, just because it was all coming to me so fast. Time for lunch, and by all means, let's explore more of the ship.

Day three: Approaching sunny Mexico

Waking up early once again, I went to the top deck and watched the ship cruise into Mexico. The once-blue waters were now green; ah, breathtaking! I thought places like this only existed in magazines or movies. After breakfast, Tina and I decided that all work and no play would make for a dull vacation. So we got up and got dressed.
We were headed off the ship to shop and explore. Since I was with her, Tina felt more comfortable exploring more of this excursion, that Mexico

had to offer, and there were a lot of beautiful part's to see.

We had a blast. It was like a second honeymoon, and the food at our resort, amazing! No more writing today; just dinner, dancing, bingo, and fun.

Day four:

For this day, Tina made sure that we copied everything that took place on her previous cruise, and boy was it a blast. Snorkeling-who knew that I had it in me? The ocean is a big and wonderful place of exploration. It's like its own underwater world. Next, adventure an ice craving challenge on a ship, really? I mean the precision that it must take to do that, how exciting. Ending the night with dinner and a little bingo and a comedy show. Cruising is amazing!

Day five:

Having the urge to research/write. But parasailing? Are you kidding me? I barely wanted to ride a roller coaster. Oh, the things that I let my wife talk me into.

Okay, so that was a blast. A bit terrifying, but fun. This has been an exciting trip. Met new friends, hung out by the hot tub, and watched a movie to close out the night. Oh boy, a mid-night buffet. The selection was incredible, and we just keep eating until we were stuffed. We should sleep well tonight.

Out-of-Body Experience

Day six:

A DAY OUT to sea. Pretty uneventful; just rest and relaxing for us both, or so I thought!

As I lay in bed this evening, I could feel the ship rocking. For some reason, I was tossing and turning. Maybe it was heartburn? Anyway, Tina reached over and hugged me. She must have noticed that I was having a hard time falling asleep. Then, in a soft, sweet voice, she said, "Is everything okay?"

I replied, "I'm fine; just trying to go to sleep."

Just by hearing her voice, I started to relax. As I began to doze off, I heard my name being called. Is that Tina again? I wondered. Then, as I opened one eye, I could see that she was sound asleep. It was clearly a woman's voice that I heard. Did she just talk in her sleep? I thought. Thinking nothing more of it, I just went back to sleep.

As I lay there, drifting to sleep, suddenly I felt myself rise upward. I see my wife lying in bed, our cabin suite, and then the top of the ship. Next, I passed through the clouds and the stars. I was fearful because I wasn't sure what was going on. Suddenly, there were bright lights, and I knew that this had to be the end for me.

"Why now am I dying God?" I said, to whomever I thought may be listening. Then I was blinded by more lights. When I was finally able to see, I was in a room. It wasn't just an ordinary room, though; it looked more like a ball-room. I noticed the walls were of a gold color and there were jewels of some sort that decorated the walls. Like any other curious person, I began to explore beyond this room. I saw a stream that was as clear as glass. The water was still and peaceful. As I walked up to it, I could see my reflection in it. I wanted to sit down and just rest by it, but I continued to walk around. I saw gold-colored streets and beautiful homes and more homes as far as the eye could see. Then I was in front of a huge table. As I looked closer, I saw many different types of foods and twelve loaves of bread.

It was as if someone was preparing for a lot of guests, a feast of sorts. As big as the table was it only had two chairs, each on opposite ends. It all seemed too familiar, and I felt like I recognized this place.

As I was about to sit in one of the empty chairs, there was a voice that came out of nowhere and said, "Charlie, those chairs are already taken." *That's weird; I don't see anyone sitting in them*, I thought. But, I certainly didn't want to argue with someone I couldn't even see. Then another voice emerged.

"Come closer. Charlie."

It was the same woman's voice that I heard right before I went to sleep. "There is another seat close to this table where you can sit."

As I walk around looking for this chair, I noticed there were twenty-four more chairs that all seemed the same and one that was different that sat just slightly off to the side.

"That's your chair, Charlie."

As I hurried over to it, my legs began to shake. I sat down.

"Don't be afraid," she said. "I can interpret the meaning of each dream that you had."

I thought, *how does she even know about my dreams?* My next thought was, *can she really make sense of my dreams? Really?* Then she continued.

"My Father knows all things. It's a fulfillment of his word spoken by the prophets. You should know that he has chosen you to help spread his word throughout the earth and help me prepare the church for the coming of our Lord and Savior, Jesus."

"I've never met you. How could I be of any assistance to you or your Father?" I couldn't help but wonder if this was her dad she was referring to. I wanted to ask her, why me? But I didn't dare speak. I felt almost lifeless but peaceful, and calm.

"Charlie, you were chosen by God to receive a revelation about his last day plans and movement. God is not finished working on the earth."

Again, I wondered how she knew about my dreams.

"You received these visions in the form of dreams. I will tell you the meaning of each. You surrendered your will, and that's why you are here today."

Was it that easy? I've been going crazy trying to figure out these dreams. had I known….

"I will now explain to you the first. You saw Eve being driven out of the garden with fire because she and Adam sinned against God's word. She wasn't with child but the pain that she experienced was symbolic of given birth to sin. Because of this, all women would now understand the pain of bearing children. God would place enmity between the serpent and all humanity. They will have a dislike for each other, even until the end of time. As her husband met her and carried her off, they were saddened to be driven out of the presence of God.

The second dream, pertained to Mary Magdalene, who loved and our Savior. She received the first visitation from Christ following his resurrection. Mary Magdalene wept immensely after Christ returned to live with his Father."

I knew it! My mom would be proud, I thought

"The third dream, was a revelation of the hidden mysteries of God. My name is written in heaven upon the throne on which I will sit. It is not yet time to reveal my name to the world, but I was sent to prepare the bride to meet Christ, and I will help crown him King of Kings and Lord of Lords. I was sent to feed God's people spiritual manna. This is food that cometh down from heaven. Within this statement is a hint or clue to my God-given name that is written upon the white stone. It is a new name, and no man knows it except he that receives it. Some refer to me as the second woman Eve; I will also be known as the feeder of God's people. I appeared unto you twice because you weren't sure if I was real, and I had a message to deliver to you. Now that you have seen, me, do you believe? You are blessed, much like Moses, to have seen hidden mysteries of God.

"The fourth dream of the woman who appeared in front of the chalkboard —that woman was Claire. She came into your life to deliver sacred writings that God , inspired her to write . She would protect these sacred writings until your meeting , and then she would provide you with the writings . You should know that God has placed many people in your life to help lead and guide you to this point , and now it's up to you to proclaim this message."

Okay, that part scared the heck out of me, so I had to ask. "I don't feel like I'm the best person for this job. I haven't live a spiritual life. Do I have to except this calling? Could I say no? We do have free agency right? How is it that God placed people in my life to help me?"

"I am sure you don't understand everything. When God places people in your life, they are there to help you. Choosing rather or not to accept them is entirely up to you, but if you refuse, then you may miss out on some of the blessings that God will have for you. John the Baptist was chosen to baptize Christ. He argued that he wasn't worthy, but this act had to come to pass, and if he refused, God would have chosen someone else. This was John's role in Christ's life, and he received many blessings by fulfilling it. Now that you are aware of your role, do not say that you are unworthy or unable to complete this task. For just as God was with his people from the beginning of time, he will also be with you. He will watch over you and protect you from hurt and danger just like he did with your accident."

Jaw dropping moment for me. "Are you telling me that God protected us in that accident?"

"Yes, Charlie, he sent his angels to stop the car from rolling over one last time. God's angels can come in the form of light and peacefulness and are dispatched at a moment's notice."

"But what about the driver that hit us?"

"Sadly, he passed away, but it is not always as it seems. He wasn't drunk as they previously thought. He was released from the hospital after suffering kidney stones. He was given a heavy dose of medicine and was told to have someone drive him home. I wish he would have listened. But he is resting peacefully. Now that you know the truth you and your wife can hopefully forgive him for his mistake." Tears were now flowing, and all I could do was shake my head.

"Charlie, on this journey you will be confronted with challenges, and the devil will try hard to stop your progress, but he will fail in his attempts if you believe. You will endure, and ultimately fulfill the calling of God, if you can just believe."

As I tried to take it all in, there was a voice from beyond like a trumpet blaring all over the place.

"The bride is ready to be received by the bridegroom. Come, Massiah, and see the marriage that will soon take place."

I was once again speechless. I saw the figure of this woman walking away and then gliding toward this bright light; I couldn't help but notice golden shoes or slippers of some kind. Not really knowing or understanding the name that he called her, I was shocked. I couldn't help but feel that time had sped forward somehow to the point that it was okay for her name to be revealed. Suddenly, there was a shaking of the room and the appearance of what looked like a man, but he was glowing and as beautiful as the morning sunrise. He stood tall and was dressed as if prepared for battle with armor on from head to toe. As he came closer, he sensed my fear.

"Fear not, Charlie. For it was I who shouted out the name of the woman seated at the table. You would not have been present to witness all of this if God didn't count you worthy. He has allowed you to partake in heavenly secrets and has permitted you to write about these things, which will come to past. It was revealed unto you the first four dreams. There were also three more. In due time God will once again make them known unto you. Now go and help spread the word of how God will do a new thing on the earth today."

Three more? I must be going crazy, I thought to myself.

Then it jumped out of my mouth. "What if no one will believe or accept these things?"

"It doesn't matter if some don't believe, Charlie. This is the will of the Almighty God! To as many as believe, God will make them his sons and daughters in Christ Jesus."

"Can you tell me the meaning of the woman's name?"

"I can tell you that she was called after the same order of Christ. The word Christ can be interpreted as "anointed one of God." A "Messiah" also means the "anointed one of God." Therefore, she will be called "Massiah "—"Messiah " represents the male of God and "Massiah " representing

159

the female side. Both were sent by God to help save, redeem

, and prepare God's people to live with him in heaven one day. Go and tell everyone who will receive this information about God's plan. Today, you have dined on heavenly food! Eat of it, and share it, for like you , those who receive it will never hunger nor thirst after righteousness again. And one day she will be revealed when you connect the ends."

All at once I was back in my bed but was not quite awake. I wanted to hear more and more, but the man was right. I felt as if I had feasted on a buffet of food, that feeling when you just want to burst. I wanted to wake my wife up, but she lay there sleeping peacefully, so I waited. As the morning approached, I couldn't get up fast enough. I spent the majority of the morning filling my wife in on the breath-taking experience that I had had last night. I mentioned to her that this man said that I somehow received three more dreams.

"Three more? Are you serious?" she yelled. (I could see her mind racing.) Then she covered her mouth as if she couldn't speak.

"Charlie," she said as her lips quivered. "I'm so freaked out right now. Do you remember how I told you that the doctor showed me some history of brain spikes that you had? Well, coincidentally, there were three of them. It all has to be connected, somehow, someway. Oh, this is all way above my pay grade. I just don't know what to say."

"I don't know, either." Now I knew that there would be more, and I craved more. "Also, Tina, it was revealed to me that the young man who hit us wasn't drunk as previously thought. He was in the hospital and had been treated for kidney stones. Apparently, they heavily medicate you sometimes for the pain. He wasn't supposed to be driving home; it was a mistake. I feel bad that I was so mad at him. But I was told that he is resting peacefully."

"That's good news to hear, Charlie. In our defense, we reacted off the information that was given to us and that was a normal reaction after hearing that a drunk driver hit you . We will continue to pray for his family."

Going Home

A T THE END of our vacation, I was still on cloud nine after what I'd seen and heard. I still couldn't believe that I had been chosen to partake in such heavenly secrets, yet I was. I could no longer contain all this information. There was still one more thing I needed to do, and that was to verify that Claire existed. Despite hearing her name called out and remembering bits and pieces of her from some writings, we needed solid proof. Having a little time to kill before our flight home, we decided to call the contact listed as Claire. I pressed the buttons. The phone rang a few times before someone answered.

"Hello?"

"Hi, can I speak to Mrs. Claire Bartlett?" "This is she."

"Ma'am, my name is Charlie Cole, and I think we may have met before." Then all at once, I heard, "Charlie? Is that you?"

Her seemingly soft voice perked up to full volume now, and the warm reception assured me that I wasn't crazy.

"Yes, this is Charlie. Ma 'am, can I ask you how we know each other?" Although I did have a strong recollection of her, I somehow wanted to convince my wife that she did exist.

"Charlie. I'm so sorry about graduation. My husband heard through some of the staff at the school that you were hospitalized and in a coma for quite some time. Given your condition, you are blessed to be alive. How have you both been? I did try and call, but your phone would go to voicemail. I prayed for you and your wife daily. I'm hope that you're doing, and feeling better."

"Thank you, ma'am. I'm still trying to piece together different events that took place before and after the accident, but I feel good."

"Please call me Claire."

"Okay. Well, Claire, my wife and I were looking through some papers that we found, and it appears that you wrote them."

Once again, the tone of her voice changed. "Oh Charlie, I've been so worried about you and your wife's well-being, but I did also wonder what became of the papers I had given you."

"Well, apparently, they are okay. While I haven't thoroughly read everything, you have some interesting titles and some insightful writings."

"Thank you, Charlie. A lot of time and effort went into writing those ten chapters."

"Ten?"

"Yes, Charlie, I gave you and your wife all of my writing. If I am correct, it equaled about ten, somewhat-completed chapters."

I didn't want to disappoint her, knowing that Tina had only four. I said, "While we were on vacation, my wife decided to bring some chapters for me to look over. I'm still in the process of reading them. I'm sure they're amazing, and I can't wait to finish."

"Oh, I hope that you like them. I feel like they were meant to be given to you both."

If it were a couple of days ago, I wouldn't have known what she meant by that. But now? I'm just glad that she didn't catch on about the missing chapters, I thought.

"Thank you, Claire. We're honored that you gave them to us."

"You're welcome. I've got to go now, but you and your lovely wife take care. God bless."

"Thank you."

Tina, now fixated on my conversation, could hardly wait for me to get off the phone.

"So, this means that she does exist, right? What exactly did she say to you?"

"Apparently she does. And I guess that confirms that neither of us is going crazy, well as far as her existence is concerned, but trying to piece everything together make me feel that way."

"Honey, I know it's all foreign to both of us right now. We've been through a lot, and we can't let whatever's happened to us in the past stop us from moving forward. There's a lot we don't remember, but that's okay. We have each other, and we're about to start a family. Let's focus on the positive things in our lives right now," she said.

The flight home was smooth and hassle-free. As we prepared for dinner that evening, I noticed that my wife was crying. I also saw that she was holding Claire's writings. I asked her why she was crying.

She replied, "It's now just sinking in. I can't get over the fact that she's real. It's just weird that I didn't remember her the first time."

"It's fine; I wasn't sure that she was real, either." She kept sorting through the papers and looking at them with disbelief. Then it hit me to check the one place, a place, where we always kept some of our essential documents: the file cabinet in the computer room. I hurried downstairs. After a brief and frantic search, I found chapters 1–5, making that a total of nine—just as Claire had said. *Wait, she mentioned ten*, I thought. I ran upstairs to show Tina what I found. She was just as thrilled as I, but then there was the missing chapter. I wasn't about to open that can of worms, at least not right now. Things were good; for the first time in a long time, things were good. One day I would find the courage to ask Claire about the missing chapter but for now I will just hope my wife doesn't bring it up.

Over the next few weeks, Tina and I read and re-read the abundance of chapters together. With every page read it seemed that we became more enlightened about the message that Claire was trying to convey. Much like Claire, we felt like we were at a standstill, and wondered what to do, or where we would start.

Time seemed to pass so quickly, and now the baby was here. What a beautiful bundle of joy, baby Linda. Watching your child come into the world-words can't describe how it feels! This amazing little human life that grew inside my wife is such a blessing to us; it feels like a miracle.

"How can you love someone that you never met so much?" I asked my wife.

"I feel the same way," she replied. Then the bombshell.

"That's how I feel about Christ," she said. "I've never met him, but I love him so much, and I know that he loves me just the same. So much, in fact, that he gave his life for me. It's a feeling that I can't explain either. It's a type of a rebirth; you feel brand new when you accept him into your life and are baptized."

My mind was blown! I stood there speechless. The meaning of her words really hit home. I thought to myself, *I would do anything to protect my daughter. Understanding just how precious life really is, there was no way I would be able to offer her up to save the world. I'm just so thankful for a healthy baby.*

As the weeks passed, it seems that we were even busier now. I was juggling my new life with a newborn, a hectic work schedule, and helping my wife recover from labor. It was going to be a challenge. Even with all that we had going on, I felt down. I thought that we had let Claire down. I wanted to have just one more dream or a message telling me exactly what the heck I was supposed to do with all of these papers. For the first time (and I mean in a very long time) I prayed for directions and answers.

Not instantly, but eventually I was given a subtle answer. Not in a loud voice. The earth didn't shake, nor did an angel of God appear to me. But I was reminded that I did get answers when I was on the ship. The explanation of my dreams that I received let me know that I was to help spread the message of the dreams, to anyone who would listen or accept them. I guess it was just that obvious!

So, a few years later I began to write and tell my story. The first chapter was...

If You Can Just Believe

IN THE BACK of my mind, I couldn't ignore the fact that I was able to hear the name of the woman called. Then I remembered what I had been told. I would have to tell this information to the world, even if some didn't believe. I became curious. I wanted to know if there were other instances throughout the Bible where mysteries or dreams were revealed, or if angels ever spoke to people with instructions from God, and much like myself; they didn't fully understand how to proceed, after their experience.

I dug out the Bible and started from the beginning. I gotten pretty good at using references and keywords to find what I was looking for.

Moses the writer of Genesis states in chapter 17,[91] "Abraham fell face down; he laughed and said to himself, Will a son be born to a man a hundred years old? And shall Sarah that is ninety years old bear?"

A child at their age? I would have had the same reaction and questioned everything, I thought.

Next I read about Noah. How crazy and insane he must have seemed to everyone when he began building an Ark as commanded by God. It had not rained in quite some time, but Noah and his family were spared because of his obedience to God's word.

I thought of Moses next, and how he saw the bush that burned but was not consumed. He was instructed to take off his shoes because the ground that stood on was holy. He faced many challenges, even after he parted the Red Sea. But he still believed and trusted in a God that he had never seen. I shuddered at the thought of what could happen to you if you accept the calling, but don't follow the plan according to how God wants you to. I guess the good news is that according to the Bible, Moses would still see a promised land. It just wasn't the one here on earth.

As I continued writing, I thought of one of the toughest cases on record, the story of Christ. He did things that defied explanation, starting with his very birth. It is almost inconceivable that God could take David's seed, preserve it down the line of time and then take that same seed and place it in a virgin woman to make a son, Matthew 1.[92] I couldn't even begin to imagine how his parents must have reacted. First, Mary was found with a child conceived by the Holy Ghost. Second, Joseph believed the angel who came to him and warned him that his wife would bear a child, and it was part of God's plan. Joseph stood by her side. He had to endure people gossiping and talking about him, not to mention he couldn't be intimate with his wife until after the child was born. Now that took some faith, trust, and belief!

Thinking about Christ himself; he had to believe what the prophets spoke concerning his life and death. He also had to believe that God was with him, how else would he be capable of performing miracles that no man had ever been able to do before? Christ needed great faith to believe that his Father would make good on his promise and not leave his soul in hell, but would resurrect him into eternal life and establish his kingdom forever.

Now, according to my dreams, it will be up to our generation to believe that God will do something new on the earth and that he will once again unite the churches and faiths. Apparently, he will send an anointed woman under his strong direction. So many won't believe because she is a woman. But God won't care. He has always come a different way than we would expect or perceive him to come or work. Her presence on earth will also become a sign that Christ will be coming back soon. She will prepare the bride for his coming, and after she's done, it will signify a completion in both heaven and earth. She will be the final mystery of God and will be declared to his servants. Just like in the days of Noah, where wickedness ran rampant through the hearts of men and God destroyed the world with water, this time he will do it with fire. (Matthew 24)[93] but he will save the righteous man from the hour of temptation that shall come upon the earth. (Revelation 3).[94]

After this chapter, I felt a little conflicted. I thought long and hard about just telling this great story from my perspective alone, or trying to paraphrase everything that I had read, heard and gone through. Ultimately, I decided that I would get an account from those who were both, directly and indirectly, involved in all my recent life experiences.

Over a brief period of time I spoke to my mother about my life. I was trying to get her perspective on what it was like watching us grow up. I also wanted to know how it felt, knowing that her son lay there near death. I can't imagine what she went through, recently becoming a father myself. I wanted to use Tina's journal entries, college papers and all the study work we did at Claire's house. I also wanted to get a first-hand account of her experiences through all of this. Last but certainly not least was Claire's. Writing. These chapters were compelling and tell a story all on their own.

Now that everything was coming together, we were faced with the daunting task of finding a title for all of this. Talk about writer's block!

I thought about something like *Charlie's life experience, Charlie's Dreams,* or perhaps *Charlie's Angels.* (I could get sued for that last one.) Again it wasn't just about me. Besides, I wanted to focus on the message being portrayed here, that Christ was the second chance for Adam, and there would be a woman who would be the second chance for Eve. After much deliberation, Tina and I couldn't agree more, this compilation of stories, experiences, and chapters would be called *'A Second Chance for Eve.'*

A Dose of Reality

A
S TINA AND I settled in for the night we planned to just sit on the couch, relax and watch a movie, but our baby had other plans and started to cry. I offered to get up and get her but Tina insisted that I get everything ready for the movie. Before I knew it, I was thinking about the events that took place on the ship and wondered how I would ever make sense of it all. As I relaxed, my body wanted, and yearned for sleep Apparently , I began to drift off into a sweet abiss. Then it happened , I had another dream.

I saw the face of a little girl playing outside with friends and siblings. Wait, are they playing with peanut-butter? *That's weird,* I thought. Next, she was jumping rope , laughing , and running around the yard .In the distance, I could see fields of hay and a few animals. The little girl was now a teenager, and I saw her reading, what appeared to be a Bible, and afterward , she knelt down to pray . She began to tell God how much she loved him. I saw her traveling to a church building in icy, rainy , snowy and very cold weather conditions . It appears that her desire to go to church and serve the Lord was extreme . I could see her traveling around a neighborhood knocking on doors and telling people about her life experiences and how she came to find Christ . Time seemed to be moving so quickly. I then saw her laying hands on a lady, praying for her to be healed from her illness in the name of our Lord and Savior (Jesus).

Through her faith and a touch from God, the lady she prayed for was healed. She began to rejoice and give thanks to God.

The dream shifted , and the young lady was now a grown woman . Judging by the ring on her left hand, I assumed that she was now married.

Then , I noticed small children running around the house ; each child would run to her, hugging her, and she would then tell them how much she loved them. I then saw this lady as she stood before a congregation and began to speak to them about her life with Christ. She began her sermon. It was titled, "Why seek ye the living among the dead? Christ has risen." She concluded, "Why you are standing around gazing into the heavens, this same Jesus that rose from the dead will return to gather his people." After she finished, the sermon, I noticed one of the parishioners come up to her, and told this lady that, "Her message was recorded in heaven."

It was as if time passed quickly somehow and I saw an older lady , but this time she was crying. I noticed a casket and a man laying inside. This must have been her husband . After the service , I could see that she was burdened with grief. As I focused on the program that she was holding I noticed the date of his service was in February. There were so many great things spoken about this man . Many people described him as a " wonderful father , a great provider , and a hard worker , who loved traveling and spending time with his family. He had a young spirit, and he was a man who loved God."

The dream shifted again. This time I saw a young man and woman sitting in the front row of a church. *Were they a brother and sister, or husband and wife? Also, where is the lady that I've been seeing?* I wondered. Many different people surrounded the two; perhaps they were family members? I once again saw a casket, and then it was as if my world stopped. This woman whom I had been seeing was now lying in this beautiful pink rose-covered casket. For some reason, I was now up in the pulpit speaking about the amazing life of this woman of God. I told about the power of prayer and how this lady fully believed in it.*Wait, I am recalling everything that I have just been shown, and how exactly do I know her?* I thought. As I continued, I told of how two brothers came face to face with a serial killer. This man approached them and asked them to carry his groceries to his

171

home and he would pay them ten dollars each. Suddenly the woman runs out of the house and yells at the man. She asked him "What are you doing?" He was startled at first and then replied.

"I hurt my back and just needed some help carrying my groceries home."

The woman said, "You're a grown man, you can carry your own stuff. And get away from my kids." The man shook, then took his groceries and ran off. The two brothers waited a few minutes and began to follow the man to see where he lived It was later determined that this killer took the lives of several kids in the neighborhood, trusting kids like us, and buried their remains under his porch. When the brothers asked their mom what made her come outside she said, "She had been praying a little earlier, and God let her know that trouble was coming so she began to check on her family first."

As I sat down, the woman from the front row went up and began telling a story. She talked about how her mother was such a spiritual person she stated, "She had a friend whose child was at the point death when her mother began to pray for the child, and just a short time later, her child was healed.

Her daughter concluded, that if that if she could only have one-half of the spiritual life experiences that her mother had, then, she would feel blessed. Many family members began to speak about this woman and described her as a fantastic cook, wife, and mother who loved a clean house. A lot of different women who came up to talk stated that she taught them how to become good wives and mothers by the examples she set. Another lady described her as an "apple of God's eye." She proclaimed that this woman had a saying "You don't have to be rich to be clean." You could tell that this woman was loved and had impacted many different lives. Toward the conclusion of the service, the minister began to eulogize her.

"This woman that lies before you had a real connection to God. Ever since she was a young child, she loved inquiring about God. She once told me that after she was baptized and began her walk with the Lord Jesus, she loved living a holy life. "Even if there were no reward (like heaven) at the end of her journey with Christ, she would still want to live holy. And she was so serious about God that she rather serve him than eat.

"I have to admit you don't see many people who are this serious about living for Christ," the minister said. He continued, "She contacted me one day about a missionary whom she had met. Her name was Rose. Lucille couldn't stop talking about this lady. She describes their meeting as 'the will of God.' She said that it was like a 'spiritual rope' was connecting her

to Rose and that everywhere she went, that she was right-behind her, 'As Rose left the room, I heard the voice of God say, 'Lucille follow me.' It was almost like the call the apostles received. I knew then that God had something special planned for my life,' she stated.

"Her life wasn't without challenges. After losing her husband of many years she became afflicted herself. She began to lose her mobility, her eyesight, and eventually her independence. She once described herself as 'Job's sister' because of everything that was coming upon her. The thing that stood out to me through all of this was she never complained about God, nor did she curse his name. I told her that our spiritual lives are types and shadows of the Bible. She asked, 'what do you mean?'

"'In our journey with Christ, some unfortunate things may happen to you much as they did to many different people throughout the bible. Your life and the things that you go through will become a type or similar situation. Or you may feel that your life shadows or mimics one of theirs as well. So if you feel like you are going through like Job, you may be. God chose him because he was the perfect and upright person to prove a point to Satan. Maybe because you chose to serve God at age sixteen and never turned back, he chose you to prove to Satan that people are still holy in this wicked world today. Your life can and will be an example and light to others.' As I spoke with her, tears began to form. And next came what I would describe as power from heaven! It took over her body, and she spoke with unknown tounges and began to praise God. She then stated, 'I thank you God for everything you have done for me in this life. I wouldn't change anything about my walk with Christ. And I know that when this life is over, I am going to that heaven that Jesus went to prepare for me. This is not just a story, but more like an example of what it means to walk with Christ, the minister concluded. And with many heavy hearts, tears, and smiles the service was over.

Looking over the program, it appear to be dated almost three years to the passing of her husband. Then I felt an extreme out pouring of emotions come over me, and sweat and tears were flowing heavily now. I wasn't even sure why I was so emotional. Suddenly I heard my name being called. "Charlie?" Followed by, "I love you, Charlie. Please always remember that." I wanted to run to the voice; it felt familiar, it felt safe, it felt like home. At first, I couldn't see who was calling me? Then I got a glimpse of this same lady, but this time she was young again. *Could this be a recollection of one, of the three dreams mentioned by the man/angel?* I thought. I suddenly woke up to my wife, Tina, holding me and the baby crying (apparently from seeing me so upset). I guess I had been crying and calling out for my mother in my sleep. Then the reality of it all sank in. I had been reliving many stories told to me by my mother, and replaying her and my father's funeral services. My heart was broken! I felt sad and alone, but I know that they were both resting peacefully . Although my life will always have a void, I know that I am blessed to have known them and shared so many life experiences together.

It was now morning and just after we woke up, we heard the doorbell ring. I was the first to get up and Tina followed. As I peeped through the glass, I noticed it was an older lady. When I opened it, there was was a familiar

174

sight. It was Claire. We welcomed her inside. She began to explain the reason for her visit. Once again she was in possession of a package. "I found another chapter, Charlie." *Ah the missing chapter*, I thought.

"It was in another box that I had at the house," Claire said. "Well, I hope that makes ten altogether." Being a former teacher meant I kept a lot of old papers around so it's no wonder I have stuff all over the place. *Thank goodness!* I thought maybe Tina and I had misplaced the last chapter." "I'm so excited for you and your wife Charlie."

Tina now joining us, began to thank her for entrusting her work to us. Claire just smiled. We showed her the progress that was made already and assured her that we would do our best to get it published. Tina rushed off to get the baby so that she could see her for the first time. Claire was overjoyed and held her for almost an hour. We had a lot to catch up on, reliving what seemed like every aspect of our lives since first meeting.

"Well, I better get going," Claire said.

"It was sure nice to see you again," Tina said.

We hugged her one more time, and then she was gone.

"There is something so special about her." I told Tina. She agreed but then asked about receiving another chapter. Before I could even answer, she said, "Never mind, Charlie, I'm sure I don't want to know the answer. I'm just glad that this is all of her work and that we finally have an idea what we're going to do with it."

From the files of Claire Chapter 10

What If?

THESE TWO WORDS, **What if,** can have you wondering and second-guessing decisions for the rest of your life. They can be thebeginning words of a million different questions.

When I was growing up, my parents tried really hard to keep us busy during the summer months. Sometimes, they would send us to summer camp, and other summers we would stay home and play with friends. One summer, our church sponsored a summer Bible study. Attending Bible study during the summer is not what the average kid looks forward to on their summer break. Thankfully, many of my friends from church wanted to attend.

Minister Reggie, our Sunday school teacher, was a lot of fun, and we were excited that he was going to teach Bible study. I wasn't sure what to call him during the summer. Anyway, at the beginning of class, he told us "This would be the best summer if we all participated in the activities." Minister Reggie then asked us for suggestions on ways to make studying the Bible fun. We looked at each other and laughed silently, as many of us didn't want to be there, or at least I didn't. So, rather than responding to his request for suggestions, we remained silent.

Since no one spoke up, he offered an idea. He said, "**What if** we viewed the Bible as a play ?" The class began to look more excited as he continued . " What are the attributes of a great theatrical play ?" He said " For example , there's a beginning , an ending and a happily ever after. The Bible is similar to a theatrical play that is filled with drama , romance , villains, and heroes," he added. "The characters in there are from all over the world. There are stories of great love and great heartbreak. Not all of the stories in the Bible will appeal to everyone, but many will. Some will touch the hearts and minds of people, while others may leave individuals pondering the meaning or moral of the story. If you look at the Bible as a play, it would be considered as the greatest theatrical play ever produced," Minister Reggie noted.

This play's story has been re-enacted by many, in theatrical performances, in college institutions, schools, and most church gatherings. What is interesting is that some would say that this play is a continued production and is still enlisting cast and supporting cast members to join. We know that this play is filled with mysteries and hidden symbolism. These mysteries have been talked about and dissected by biblical experts, yet there will be just a few who understand its true meaning."

This was new and creative, so we began to play along. As we would come, each day there would be scriptures written on the chalkboard of the Sunday School-now-turned-summer classroom. Each of us would take turns reading the scriptures in dramatic fashion. Some would speak with an accent that they believed best portrayed that time period or character they With about a month to go, our director presented a new challenge that went along with what we were doing. He wanted us to think about three of the most intriguing characters in the Bible, and we would spend the rest of the time learning about them.

As we sat around and debated a bit, the first one that we all agreed upon who was by far the most intriguing was God himself. While Enoch made a strong case by being translated , we chose two others, and they were Melchizedek and Jesus Christ.

Our director was on board with this, so we started with God. Yes the creator himself, of not only the heavens and earth but of humanity as well.

We discovered many interesting facts. First, God is so amazing, and it is almost impossible to contemplate why or even how he does what he does. Also, to even think about where he came from will drive you crazy. Our director informed us that many people believed that God was all three of the people that we had chosen. So, we began to ask ourselves, **What if** God was all three?

Since many may not be familiar with these characters, I wanted to kind of focus on the part where this great God could have been Melchizedek. Although there is much mystery surrounding him, many people believe that Melchizedek existed and was in fact someone very special.

This character (Melchizedek) is said to have just appeared, having no beginning of days nor ending of life. What a suitable role for God; coincidentally he too has no beginning of days no ending of life. Melchizedek is discussed over a period of 2,100 years, starting when he first appeared to Abram in Genesis 14[95]. You see, in this part God himself could have taken on a human bodily form. Why, one may ask? The answers can be found in the latter part of verse 18. It states that Melchizedek was the priest of the highest God. It didn't say a priest but the priest. There appears to be a play on words here. The word the is more specific to one person. The priest of the most high, that has to be God himself in a form. The letter A, used in this context means another or more than one, like another high priest, so that meant that there was already one! The other thing that is going on is God's word is establishing a holy eternal priesthood here because of the failure of humanity. Now we travel down the line of time to where Melchizedek is mentioned again.

In the book of Psalms 110, [96] we find the writer speaking about David and his son Jesus, but also referencing Melchizedek. "The LORD (God) hath sworn, and will not repent, Thou art a priest forever after the order of Melchizedek."

When you speak of the word order, to us it means to follow a certain established pattern, but it's defined as the arrangement or disposition of people or things in relation to each other according to a sequence, pattern, or method.[97] So, Jesus would follow this same pattern of an eternal priesthood. Lastly, in Hebrews 7, [98] it indicates once again that Melchizedek had no mother or father or descent (having ancestry or family). Verse 3 continues "But made like unto the son of God abideth a priest continually." Verse 4, "Now consider how great this man was." So, it's calling Melchizedek a great man. We know that God is a spirit, so for him to play this part, he would take on the form of a man. In verse 15 it states, "And it is far more evidence for that after the similitude of Melchizedek there ariseth another priest." So when you look at the word *similitude*, it is defined as, the quality or state of being similar to something. It also means resemblance, similarity, likeness, sameness, similar nature, comparability, correspondence, comparison.[99]

However, there was some controversy as many speculate that Melchizedek was a character named Shim. Although Shim lived a long life, he had a beginning of life and ending of life. Someone else said that it had to be one of God's holy angels. That would be a very good guess as well. Now, God's angels are eternal beings, they had beginning of days, when God himself created them. So the only one who has never had no beginning to him nor will ever have end of life is God himself, even though we don't understand why he would take on a form and come down to visit humanity. **What if**, that's exactly what he did through Melchizedek?

As we travel just a little further in time, **what if** this great God once again played a major role; this time he would be his son. There was so much literature available about the son of God that it made my head spin. I then enlisted the help of my director to explain **what if** God could have starred in this role. He said for this to be possibly the story would have to read like this. "Therefore, God took the seed of David and preserved it all that time. He got in the seed and placed it inside of Mary and then, yes, God also was

179

in Mary's stomach and would grow there for nine months and experienced childbirth.

God then was this little holy child that was nursed by his mother as he grew up. He was in a house-hold with other siblings, and no doubt God was disciplined for getting into trouble for perhaps fighting with his brother. He slept and ate as a human child needs to. He also needed to bathe because flesh can get dirty Now God would grow up studying about himself and later tell his mother that he needed to be about his own business). He continued, God would hear about how he would take away the sins of the world and how he would be crucified to do so. God would then cause himself to be baptized to receive the Holy Spirit of himself so that he could do this production. In Matthew 3^{100} God performed a ventriloquist act by making his own voice come from heaven saying, "This is my beloved son/self, in whom I am well pleased."

God would meet up with many different men whom he would have by his side to learn of him. He would teach them about his character (his son/himself) so that they could believe in him. On one occasion, God can be found sleeping in the midst of a terrible storm, where the men on board though that they were going to die. When they woke God, he tells them to have faith, and he rebukes the winds and calms the storm. They were so baffled by having God in their mist that later on Peter, as a regular man, dared to ask God if he too could walk the waters.

Then you fast forward to what is called the last supper, or Passover. There God is telling his disciples how he will be betrayed and offered up as a sacrifice for cleansing the world from sin.

God heard about his death and realized that the time had come . God would go into the garden and pray to himself to change his mind about how he would have to die. He would pray to himself three times , each more frantic than the other. He was in character so much that sweat began to fall like great drops of blood. He wanted to show his disciples that he was praying to himself, even though they fell asleep. After not answering himself, for the third time, he got up and told himself, not my will but, my will be done. And he as the almighty God, required his created angels to come down and assist him with the strength to complete his journey. This would prove to be the climax. God would then be arrested and travel from judgment hall to judgment hall , and the people would choose Barabbas to set free instead of God.

God was then nailed to the cross and hung there to die like a sinner, even though he did not sin. As the hour of his death drew near God would be pierced in his side. God would then cry out to himself, "Myself, myself, why hast thou forsaken myself?"[101] God then cried with a loud voice and yielded up the ghost. Then God died! But on the third day, God rose himself from the grave and later ascended into the heavens to sit on the right side of himself."

This is where our project/play ended. It was a fun summer, just like my director said it would be. I made new friends and learned a lot. I really got to view the Bible in a whole new light.

However, later in life, I received a true understanding of the word of God, I know that even though the Bible seems like a production or a play and it was fun viewing that way, there are many biblical truths. I also discovered that there are many biblical scriptures that just didn't coincide with the **what if** scenario, when it came to God playing the part of Jesus. Sadly that is what is being taught in churches all over the world. Why would God go through all that trouble to play the part of his son in real life?

I just didn't want to tell you how crazy that thought was; I wanted to explain how I came to the knowledge of the truth. Why would God wrap himself up in the flesh and come down as his son Jesus and dwell with man? Better yet, why would he dwell in a woman 's stomach ? Would he just want to experience childbirth , and the same hard labor that he cursed women with because of Eve? He would then have to be born into sin, because that's how every child born of a woman comes into this world. He would portray his son to show us how to live holy. God is already holy; he knows no other way to live. But we are human; we have flaws. We would need his spirit to help us overcome our flesh and live holy. That is one of the main reasons that God sent his son into the world so that we could overcome our flesh and the sins that are in the world. In fact, it would be outright trickery for God to tell us that we can be like his son, knowing all along that it was himself. Do I dare say if that were the case, where God was his son, then that would make everything that Jesus, his Father, and the Bible said a lie!

First, the above mentioned where Jesus was baptized and received the Holy Ghost, and the voice from heaven said, "This is my son, in whom I am welled pleased." Why would the Bible say in Hebrews 4,102 "For we have not an high priest which cannot be touched with the feeling of our infirmities, but was in all points tempted like as we are yet without sin?" God cannot be touched by our infirmities and he cannot be tempted, nor will he ever tempt any man.

Speaking about a high priest, there were some similarities between Christ and Melchizedek. They were both men, but with some obvious differences. The biggest one is that Christ was born of a woman, Mary. He had an earthly father, David and a stepfather, Joseph, while Melchizedek had no mother or father. However, Christ would be called after the same order. I would also like to draw your attention to the scripture that was mentioned in Hebrews 7. "But made like unto the son of God abideth a priest continually." This right here tells us that Melchizedek, when he appeared, was made flesh like the son of God; Again, God would be taking on a form here. Also, there is that word *made*, which means there is a maker.

People get confused by the miracles that Jesus performed, and they want to make him the eternal God. Now, you have to understand that God gave Jesus the power to perform such miracles. If you never see and understand that Jesus was a man, you will always have an excuse never to try and do the works that he did, when he said, "Greater works shall you do."

This is the important thing to remember if you are seeking for true answers. God doesn't play games. Really, if God pulled this off, it would be the greatest acting job ever. He wouldn't go through all of this to fool us. What would he accomplish? Would he do this to show us his greatness, or how to live holy? He created the world, so we know that he is great. He can't sin, so that's what makes him holy. Jesus came to take away not only the sins of the world but the excuses, too. In the end, I could stand before God on that Day of Judgment and say, God, you have never been tempted by the devil to do evil. How could you know what it feels like? He has never been sick unto death or had to deal with diseases. I know that God has feelings because he cares deeply for humanity. So much that he gave his son's life to save ours

God said in Peter 3,[103] that "He would that no man should perish but come to repentance." He has to have some different type of feelings so that he can make the tough decisions that we would never want to make, such as who lives or dies. But at the same time, he is just and justified in making those decisions. Remember, he had to make the biggest decision of all choosing to sacrifice his one and only son to save us. That couldn't have been easy. Jesus had to come in the flesh. Jesus had to be born just like us. Some 2,000 years later, technology has caught us with the miracle that God performed on Mary. Facilities can take the seed of a man, place it in a woman, and she can conceive a child. Yes, they can even determine the sex of the child and place twins in her as well. Isn't God great, giving humanity knowledge to perform this? In closing, the Bible answers a very important question.

What is the will of God? The answer is in John 6.[104] "And this is the will of him that sent me, that everyone which seeth the Son, and believeth on Him, may have everlasting life: and I will raise him up at the last day." We know that not everyone can physically lay eyes upon Christ because we have different time periods. But we see him for who he is, a man tempted like you and me. But you also must believe on him as the scriptures have said. And that is the true will of God.

The End

About The Author

NATE GALVIN IS a resident of Utah and is married with four children. He currently attends Southern New Hampshire University, where he is majoring in business. *A Second Chance for Eve?* is his debut novel , but stay tuned for a follow up book The *Second Woman Eve Revealed.*

A Message from The Author

I would like to, personally, thank each of you for purchasing *A Second Chance for Eve.* I hope you enjoyed reading it, as much as I enjoyed writing this book. I would like to inform you that my book is now available in e-Book format. And coming soon, audio book, as well as Apple I-tunes, and Google play.

A Second Chance for Eve is a tribute to some very special people. These individuals had a significant impact on my life, and the lives of many others, and even acknowledging them on my "Special Thanks" page, cannot fully express my gratitude for their commitment and contributions to helping me to become the person I am today.

Charlie, the main character, was named after my late father, Charles. Charlie was his nickname. My mother, Lucille, is portrayed in the book as Charlie's mother. In fact, even the smallest details and descriptions of Charlie's mother, accurately reflect my mother, Lucille. She was an amazing woman! She had nine children, whom she loved dearly. She always had an encouraging word to lift your spirits, a hug when you were feeling down, and a smile that would light up any room. 'Lou, Lou,' as she was affectionately called by my father, loved God more than life, itself, and served him until he called her home to be with him.

The "Church Meeting" that Charlie's mother spoke about in the book was a real-life event that took place in early 1960's. The late Dr. Rosemary Cosby, also known as (Mama), is portrayed as the character, Rose, in the story. Mere words cannot describe how special this lady is/was to all that knew her. I can, honestly, say that she was one of the most spiritual individuals that I have ever had the privilege of meeting. Mama wasn't a "do as I say pastor", but she led by example. Her "Holy-Ghost filled life" made you want to also live Holy, and free from sin. After being called to the ministry, she began seeking God for answers. Mama felt that many denominations, including in the Pentecostal religion, had strayed from the teaching of the Apostles, and left truth lying in the streets. She declared that her church wouldn't give God any rest until he rained righteousness in the earth. Like God did with the Apostle, Peter and the Apostle, Paul, he revealed his son, Jesus Christ to her-showing her that he was a man, tempted like all of us-yet without sin.

Mama's message to the world was, "We must get back on the foundation that was laid by the Apostles, with Jesus being the chief corner stone."

When categorizing this book, I labeled it fictional, but it is rooted in biblical truths. It beckons to answer many questions like, "Does God intend to use another woman to redeem Eve, just as he did with Christ, who was called second man Adam from glory ? Has this discovery / revelation been hidden from others, even biblical scholars? Could these hidden mysteries change women's roles in Christianity?"

I wanted to extend to my readers an opportunity to visit, and follow my Face Book page, titled, *A Second Chance for Eve?* On this page, I will be uploading a series of videos where friends, family members, and myself will answer many of your questions , and cover the book chapter by chapter.

I invite you to share this book with your friends and family. We know that provocative and suggestive books sell millions of copies, let's show the world that good, clean, Christian books, not only have a place in our society , but there is a need for these types of books in the publishing industry.

Bibliographic

Miller, Kenneth. "Finding Darwin's God."First edition (1999) Harper Collins PS Edition (2007) http://www.findingdarwinsgod.com/

Brown, Dan. "The Da Vinci Code." New York; Doubleday, April 2003 Danbrown.com

Biography.com Editors "Mother Teresa," A&E Television Networks, *The biography.com website, September 6, 2016* http://www.biography.com/people/mother-teresa-9504160

Biography.com Editors "Oprah Winfrey" A&E Television Networks *the Biography.com*

Website. Access date January 12, 2017, http://www.biography.com/people/oprah-winfrey-9534419

Webster's Dictionary 10th Edition https://www.google.com/#q=meaning+of+the+word+influential http://www.biblehub.com/

[1]Kenneth, Miller. "Finding Darwin's God." First edition (1999) Harper Collins PS Edition (2007) www.findingdarwinsgod.com

[2]Dan, Brown "The Da Vinci Code." New York; Doubleday, April 2003 Danbrown.com

[3]Isa. 43:19 King James Version 4 Matt. 11:25

[4]Matt. 11:25

[5]Mark 10:40

[6]Rev 10:7

[7]Rev 13:8

[8]Jer. 1:7

[9]John 19:34

[10]Matt. 20:20-23

[11]1 Cor. 15:45

[12]2 Sam. 7:12

[13]1 Cor. 15:39

[14]James 1:13

[15]Matt. 5:17

[16]Mat 26:39

[17]Gen 3:19

[18]Gen. 2:16

[19]Gen. 3:18

[20]Ps. 69:21-22

[21]Act 2:27

[22]Pet. 4:6

[23]Gal. 3:13

[24]Rev. 21:3

[25]Gen. 1:26

[26]Gen. 1:27

[27]Webster's Dictionary 10th edition (2000)

[28]John 1:18

[29]John 14:8

[30]Webster's Dictionary 10th edition (2000)

[31]Dan. 3:25

[32]Phil. 2:6

[33]Webster Dictionary 10th edition (2000)

[34]Matt. 5:48

[35]John 3:2

[36]John 16:33

[37]Gen. 1:27

[38]John 3:3

[39]John 3:4

[40]Num. 20:7-9

[41]Gen. 2:17

[42]Mark 10:40

[43]Matt. 16:19

[44]Matt. 2:16

[45]Exod. 33:19-23

[46]Exod. 34:28

[47]Gen. 24:65

[48]2 Chron. 3:14

[49]Exod. 3:1-7

[50]John 14:8-9

[51]John 14:10-11

[52]John 1:1-14

[53]Cor. 6:19

[54]John 2:19

[55]2 Sam. 7:1-29

[56]1 Chron. 22:1

[57]John 2:19

[58]Acts 1:4-5

[59]https://www.google.com/#q=meaning+of+the+word+influential

[60]Ruth 1:1-16

[61]Ruth 4:13

[62]Esther Chapters 1-4, 4-16

[63]Biography.com Editors "Mother Teresa," A&E Television Networks, The biography.com website, September 6,2016 http://www.biography.com/people/mother-teresa-9504160

[64]Biography.com Editors "Oprah Winfrey" A&E Television Networks the Biography.com website Access date January 12, 2017 http://www.biography.com/people/oprah-winfrey-9534419

[65]Matt. 25:1-13

[66]Matt 24:42

[67]Rev. 19:7

[68]Rev. 21:2

[69]Rev. 21:9-11

[70]Joel 2:28

[71]Isa. 46:19

[72]2 Cor. 12:4

[73]Rev. 10:4

[74]Col. 1:26-27

[75]Heb. 7:11-15

[76]Heb. 5:5-6

[77]Matt. 11:25

[78]James 1:5

[79]Webster's Dictionary

[80]Matt 5:8

[81]John 1:18

[82]John 14:9

[83]John 1:11

[84]Acts 11:18

[85]Rev 19:16

[86]Ps. 110:1

[87]Rev. 19:7

[88]John 1:11-13

[89]Rev. 2:17

[90]Joel 2:28

[91]Gen. 17:17

[92]Matt. 1:18

[93]Matt. 24:38

[94]Rev. 3:10

[95]Gen 14:18

[96]Psalms 110:4

[97]Webster Dictionary

[98]Hebrews 7:1-17

[99]Webster Dictionary

[100]Matt 3:17

[101]Matt 27:46-50

[102]Heb 4:15

[103]Peter 3:9

[104]John 6:40